I0570595

Were Chronicles

PACK SECURITY

CRISSY SMITH

Pack Security
ISBN # 978-1-78686-378-2
©Copyright Crissy Smith 2018
Cover Art by Cover Cherith Vaughn ©Copyright September 2018
Interior text design by Claire Siemaszkiewicz
Totally Bound Publishing

PACK SECURITY

Dedication

For my girl — always believe.

Chapter One

Cassandra Wilson pushed open the bedroom balcony doors and stepped out into the cool morning air. The bite of the wind was sharp, but it cooled down her heated body. The bad dreams and sense of betrayal had her feeling ill.

She was still reeling from the events of the night before. Someone had broken into her studio and destroyed...everything. Hours of hard work ripped, torn, and broken to litter the floor. It'd appeared as if a tornado had gone through to ruin every piece she'd put her heart and soul into.

Her evening had started so normal but the end... Tears pricked her eyes again. After she'd eaten dinner with her brothers, sister-in-law and nephews, they'd taken the horses for a ride. The journey through the canyon had been freeing and she'd enjoyed the time with her family. It was nights she was able to spend in nature that helped feed her muse. Cassie knew she saw things differently from other people and believed she was blessed. On the back of her horse, she felt a connection to the world around her almost like when she was shifted. Even a short ride normally had Cassie so motivated that she'd spend the entire night in her studio.

But the previous night hadn't gone as planned. The glorious sunset and warm sensations she'd had after their ride had vanished when she'd opened her studio door and seen the destruction. Her canvases had been torn and ripped, paint splattered over the floor and walls, and every brush had been broken in half.

She had a security system and cameras but had forgotten to set them that evening. Everything that had been ruined was really her fault. Alex was forever getting on to her about remembering to set her alarm, but in the middle of the Pack territory, Cassie never worried. Now her whole life had been destroyed.

It wasn't just the loss of months of work that bothered her. She felt violated. And scared.

A knock on her bedroom door interrupted her, but she ignored it. She just wanted to be alone. Was that too much to ask? She didn't want to go to her workspace and nor did she want to talk to anyone. The police, her family, her assistant, even some of the Pack had shown up the night before. While she appreciated their support and concern, they just didn't understand. Someone had been in her house. Since her studio was located in her residence, there was no place that seemed untouched. A stranger could have gone through her things before tearing apart her creations.

She didn't know what to do now, how to act or what to say.

Her first instinct had been to hide, covers over her head, and cry, but she knew that wouldn't solve anything. As much as she wanted to pretend nothing had happened, she'd gotten up and showered to start the day. Cassie had made it as far as walking to the balcony to stare out at the territory she called her own. But that was as far as she'd made it. She just couldn't force herself to go into her studio yet.

The rapping on her door grew louder and more persistent. She suspected it was her older brother. When the door opened and Alex called her name, she sighed. Her solitude was over.

"Hey," he said as he joined her on the balcony.

Cassie glanced over her shoulder. "Hi."

"You okay?" He groaned. "That's a stupid question. I'm sorry. But what can I do to make things okay?"

She turned back to look at the sun rising above the canyon. That was the question all right. What could she do? Or Alex? Or any of them. It wasn't just Cassie who was suffering. This was the home of their family. A home they'd protected for generations.

They were lucky. The Wilson ranch was one of the few privately owned properties that shared the public canyon land. The estate had belonged to their family long before the government had come in and sectioned off acreage for a national park.

The government had tried to claim their property, too, but years of legal battles had ensured that the Wilson land would stay in the family. Cassie got to rouse every morning to one of the most beautiful views in the world. Even after the night of heartbreak she'd experienced, there was nothing like standing outside and watching the earth wake up. Alex leaned against her and she soaked up the warmth coming from him. Her oldest brother might have a tendency to hold on too tight at times, but she appreciated it more than he'd ever know. Cassie wasn't like others in the Pack. She wasn't as outgoing and was most at peace inside her studio with a paintbrush in her hand. "I don't know what to do."

"I just got off the phone with the Alpha," Alex told her. "We have a meeting with him this morning about how to handle this situation."

Knowing that she couldn't avoid the issue any longer, she turned and gave her brother her full attention. He'd set two mugs onto the rail and she hadn't noticed. She smiled and relieved him of one of the cups. The scent of fresh, strong coffee drifted up and she was grateful. She was extremely dependent on caffeine to carry her through long days.

"What time?" she asked before taking a drink. Flavor burst over her tongue—she knew her sister-in-law must have made the coffee that morning. Alex tended to make his more sludge-like.

"An hour," he replied.

So soon. Which made sense, because their Alpha would want to make sure she was safe. The traits that made her Alpha such a great leader were always right on the surface. Alpha Shawn was strong, dedicated, and fierce. She couldn't have wished for a better protector.

"You're going to get tired of everyone asking you if you're okay," Alex commented. "Just remember that we do it because we love you."

To have time to phrase her answer correctly, she took another long drink. Her brother always worried. He said it was because as the eldest, so he was responsible for her and their younger brother, Jacob. Cassie just thought he was a worry wart.

"I'll be fine," she assured him.

"Cas." There was a growl in his tone.

"I just don't understand. Why would someone break in and destroy my stuff?" She shook his head. "Why? Alex, I've never done anything to anyone."

"Fuck." Alex kissed the top of her head. "I want to tear out the throat of whoever did this."

That shouldn't make me feel good, should it? Instead of trying to get her brother to calm down, Cassie wanted to sic him on whoever had invaded her privacy. But she had to be an adult. "Is it because...we're shifters?"

"Hopefully, we'll find out. Alpha Shawn is concerned about the publicity you've gotten lately. That's one of the reasons he wants to meet."

Publicity? She snorted. Most artists wanted to receive credit for their work. All Cassie had ever needed was to paint. Her parents had supported her through the beginning stages and after their death, Alex had continued with encouragement. She'd made a good living, then the shifters had announced their presence and became public. There had been a surprising demand for her work after that.

The strangest part to her was that the Pack hadn't gone public with the others. Alpha Shawn had decided to remain in secret. The fact that her art was considered as an authentic representation of the shifter world by both humans and shifters was surprising.

And a little uncomfortable.

The press constantly pressured her about her knowledge of shifters. She'd gotten to the point where she didn't do interviews anymore. She just wanted to paint. She didn't really care about the rest of it.

"I never meant to draw attention to us."

Alex hugged her. "Ah, honey, there's nothing to be done about it. I'm proud of you. So is our Alpha. We'll get to the bottom of this and it'll all work out. I promise."

She wanted to believe him, but the wound was too fresh. She hoped Alpha Shawn had some ideas. He was one of the smartest men she knew and just a tad devious.

"I spoke to James also," Alex said. "He's going to bring over everything we have in storage and order more supplies for you. We'll have you back to work before you know it."

Cassie always had back-up supplies. She lived in the guesthouse and her studio was one of the rooms. At the main house, where Alex lived, he kept a supply room for her so she didn't have to have an order rushed to her.

"I'm almost ready for the show anyway." She was supposed to be having a showing in less than a month. "If we even still have it."

"We'll have it," Alex said. "I told you not to worry about it."

She nodded and stopped herself from telling him she was going to worry anyway. The threat they'd received in the mail to stop the show or else still weighed on her mind. Even though everyone told her it wasn't her fault, she knew it was. The crazy Church that had been after the shifters for months now had narrowed in on her town.

"We'll talk about it with Alpha Shawn. He is aware of the threat and has Chase looking into it."

"Okay," she relented. It was never worth arguing with Alex. He would eventually get his way by wearing her down. Hopefully Shawn could talk some sense into him. He was one of the few people Alex listened to.

"Let's go then." Her brother motioned her back inside.

Cassie followed him through her bedroom and into the hallway. Her house consisted of four bedrooms, a living room, a kitchen and a small fenced-in area for a backyard. The guesthouse was just yards away from the main residence where Alex lived.

Alex hadn't even wanted her this far, though. He'd tried to talk her into just remodeling a portion of the main residence, but Cassie needed space. She was an adult and way past living under the same roof as her brother. Plus, she'd gotten to design the entire place. She loved every inch of her home. And she was close enough to her brothers, sister-in-law and nephews to see them every day.

Jacob and Peyton resided a couple of miles down the hill in their own home. They had a nice six-bedroom dwelling that fit their family perfectly. Jacob worked for the Parks and Wildlife Department stationed in the canyon. Peyton stayed home and took care of their boys, one aged four and one aged six. Cassie enjoyed having her family so close to her most of the time. However, she would've preferred a little more distance right then. Alex strolled through her place like he belonged there. She didn't comment as she followed him. Normally Alex tried to show her that he respected her space, although once in a while, he went overprotective on her.

Since she'd found the destruction the night before, Alex had been in full alpha male mode. She would never admit it to him, but his protectiveness was easing some of her fear.

The drive to the Alpha compound took thirty minutes. Shawn lived deeper in the canyon. If they'd taken the horses, it would have only been ten minutes.

Not all members of the pack lived inside the canyon. Most had houses and businesses in town. Only the oldest families had claim to any canyon land.

As he drove, Alex talked about the horses and his upcoming plans for the ranch. Cassie had heard it all before, so she was able to tune him out and respond with some sounds.

By the time they arrived at the large Alpha cabin, she'd almost fallen asleep. She'd barely slept at all the previous night and was bone-tired. The winding roads that led to the house, and the familiar trip, soothed her further.

Her brother stopped the truck and patted her knee. "Let's get this over with, then you can get some real sleep. I can tell you didn't get a wink."

"Yeah, okay," she agreed and pushed her door open.

There were other vehicles parked nearby, but that wasn't a surprise. She'd never been to Alpha Shawn's when the house didn't have several guests. Having all those Pack members around would drive her crazy. She couldn't stand to have people constantly underfoot. It was one of the other reasons she lived in the guesthouse instead of the main home. Alex worked from home, and Cassie couldn't handle all the people who came in and out to do business with him.

The door opened before they reached it and her Alpha stepped out. Shawn Mathewson stood on the porch and opened his arms. He was an attractive man with dark skin and hair, his eyes and smile dazzling her. The power that rolled off him could be quite intimidating, but he was truly a good man and a great leader.

She grinned and walked up the stairs where her Alpha engulfed her. He held her tightly then patted her shoulder.

Taking a step back, she peered up at the impressive man in front of her. Just being in his presence helped calm the wolf inside her, which had been agitated since she'd found the break-in.

"Let's go inside," he said, placing his arm around her shoulder.

They entered his home and went through to the living room. Cassie saw the Beta of the pack, Chase Lawson. She inclined her head toward him in respect.

"Hey, sweetie," he greeted. "You doing okay?"

Cassie nodded. "As well as can be expected."

"We'll find out who did this."

A promise that she knew Chase would do his best to keep. The Lawson family had been part of the Pack for as long as hers had. Chase owned the local diner and was one of the best cooks in the area. She made a point of stopping by for home-cooked meals as often as possible.

He always greeted her with a smile and a kind word. He was Alex's age and the two had grown up together as the best of friends since they'd started school.

Chase welcomed Alex with a hug and a manly slap on the back while Alpha Shawn moved Cassie to the couch, taking a seat with her. Alex sat across from her in one of the chairs and, after making four mugs of coffee, Chase passed them around before he joined them.

Cassie placed both hands on the large cup as she settled back in the corner of the couch. She felt protected and secure with the three men. If she closed her eyes, she had no doubt she would be fine.

Their voices flowed over her as they discussed who could have been responsible and why. Cassie couldn't imagine anyone who would have wanted to destroy her work. Even with the shifter controversy, she was only an artist.

"We're just guessing here." Alpha Shawn's words drew her out of her thoughts. "And until we get to the bottom of this, the entire Pack will be on high alert. I don't want anyone alone. I'll double the guards around town and here."

"Cassie can stay at the main house," Alex added.

"Wait!" She sat up straight. "I'm not moving out of my house."

Three sets of eyes turned to her.

"No." She shook her head. "I have to work hard to make up for the canvases that I lost."

"It's just temporary," Alex assured her.

"I'll set the alarm. I'm sorry I forget. And we have the cameras."

"Cass." Alex leaned forward and braced his forearms on his knees. "It's more than that. We don't know who or why someone did this. Luckily, you weren't home but…"

Cassie saw the struggle on his face. He was concerned about her.

She set her mug down and spoke directly to him. "But if I just move to the main house, then they win."

"This isn't about winning! This is about keeping you safe!"

Cassie ignored the rise of Alex's voice. "I'm not giving up my house."

"Yes, you are!"

"Hold on!" Alpha Shawn tried to interrupt.

"No, I'm not. I'm a big girl and I can take care of myself."

Alex rose and towered over her. "You…are…staying in the main house." Each word was clipped.

She seldom argued with him, but she just couldn't give in this time. She'd worked hard to gain her independence after their parents' death. She was thirty years old and refused to be treated like she was five.

"No."

Alex stepped forward, but Chase stood and got between them. "How about a compromise?"

Both she and Alex turned to him.

Chase motioned Alex back down and waited until he had settled again before taking his own seat.

"What's your idea?" Alpha Shawn asked.

"Well, you know Max is back. He's working in the diner right now, but we can use him as Cassie's personal security."

Max Lawson, Cassie mused. She hadn't seen Chase's elder brother in a long time. He was older than both Alex and Chase so Cassie hadn't been around him much growing up. By the time Max had left the Pack at seventeen to join the Navy, she'd only been seven. She knew about him because he was the Pack's only non-shifter. Not that he was human. Max was a shifter. He carried the DNA that made them different from humans. However, Max was unable to shift into his animal. Cassie didn't know much about non-shifters, but Alpha Shawn had never allowed Max to be treated any differently, from what she could remember.

There were rumors about Max being part of one of the elite Navy Seal teams in the military, but that could have been all talk.

Alpha Shawn was smiling. "I like that idea."

Cassie wasn't so sure. "I don't really think I need personal security. I hardly even leave the property." She just didn't feel right about having someone follow her around all the time. Yes, the situation was scary, but assigning a bodyguard? It was a little too much.

"I disagree," her Alpha said. "The break-in was at your residence. Max would be able to keep an eye on you and look into who might have been responsible."

She knew the expression on his face. Alpha Shawn had made up his mind.

"I'll spend most of my time in the studio anyway," she argued. "He'll be in my way."

Chase chuckled. "I promise he won't."

Knowing she was coming up against a wall, she sighed. "This is stupid."

Alpha Shawn reached over and patted her knee. "Then just humor me. I want you safe."

"Fine." She rolled her eyes. She would make the best of the situation—she always did. Besides, how bad could it be? Chase was a good guy, so she doubted that Max was much different.

* * * *

Max Lawson pulled the skillets off the stove then dropped them into the sink full of soapy water. He stretched his arms over his head and rolled his neck. He liked working at the Canyon Café with his brother, even if it was dissimilar from what he had always done before. The most important thing was that he had something to do. He could concentrate on a task and not have to think or remember.

Not having enough to do worried him and made him nervous, so he was glad for the hard work.

"Hey, Max!"

He glanced over his shoulder and saw his brother in the doorway. "Hey, bro."

His brother had been summoned to the Alpha house earlier that morning, leaving Max to handle the breakfast rush for him.

"Got a minute?" Chase tilted his head, indicating that Max should join him out front.

"Sure." Max turned and followed him out of the kitchen into the dining area.

The rush was over. Only a few customers were still eating. Sue Ellen was taking care of the patrons, so Max didn't have to worry about them. He always liked being in the back more than waiting tables.

He'd only been home about six months, so when the Pack members saw him, they wanted to know about his time away. And Max honestly couldn't talk about it. Too much of what he'd done was still classified.

Chase took a seat on one of the chairs in front of the counter, next to another man. Max followed but remained back where the scarred countertop separated them. He still didn't like to be too close to people.

Once he reached the two, he recognized Alex Wilson. Chase and Alex had remained tight, even as the years passed and they'd found different interests. Max grinned at Alex and offered his hand. "Nice to see you again, Alex."

They shook hands and Alex smiled. Max tucked his hands behind his back. Just the small, polite gesture of shaking was hard. He didn't want Chase to see his struggles, though. Being Beta of the pack was hard enough. At least he got to share the role with Alex, the two of them having someone by their sides. It reminded Max of how he'd been with the men in his unit. The men he'd promised to protect.

"You too. Glad you made it back safe."

Max nodded but didn't say anything. Yes, he had returned safely, but… No, he couldn't think about that now. Instead, he noticed his brother's obvious worry. Max offered Chase a small smile before giving his full attention to Alex.

The Wilson family was one of the oldest members of the Pack. Chase, of course, was closer to them, living as a Pack, but Max still had a connection with the family. He'd been out of the country when he'd received word that the Wilson parents had been killed in an accident.

Chase had been devastated and had told him how hard it had been on the kids. It seemed Alex had stepped up and done a good job getting his siblings through the grieving process.

"Coffee?" Max picked up the pot from under the counter.

Chase and Alex nodded.

He poured three cups then slid the first two across to them. "So, what's going on?"

They exchanged a look that stood the hair up on the back of Max's neck. "What?"

"We need your help," Alex said.

"Of course," he offered. He would do whatever he could to help any of the Pack members. Even though he hadn't quite fit in with the kids growing up, they had never been mean to him. Their Alpha would not have allowed it.

Max didn't understand why he was different from everyone else. What had gone wrong to make him unable to shift? But it was what it was and there was nothing he could do about it.

"Good." Chase drew his attention. "Do you remember Cassandra?"

"Your younger sister?" he asked Alex. He could picture the freckle-face girl with skinned knees, running around in shorts. She had always been tagging behind Alex and Chase as the boys had grown up. "Sort of."

Alex nodded. "We need security for her."

"Why?"

As Alex and Chase filled him in on what was going on, Max found himself growing angry. He knew he had to get a handle on his reaction, though. After his last mission, he had gone through a debriefing and had been shown several techniques to control himself. The military did not want him to go off on civilians.

But the thought of anyone threatening a member of his Pack made his blood boil. He listened intently as Alex explained the entire situation.

"What do you need from me?" he asked when the man was finished.

"Cassie won't agree to move into the main house. She wants to stay in her residence and studio. I'm not comfortable with her being alone."

"You want me to watch over her?" he asked, surprised. He wasn't a guard. He didn't have a position with the Pack. His brother was the Alpha's second, his Beta, but after Max had left for the Navy, he'd given up any rank within the Pack.

"Yes," Chase answered. "Alpha Shawn agreed. We're doubling all security for the Pack, but we want Cassie to have someone with her full-time."

Max owed his Alpha a lot for always supporting him. Hell, he owed his brother, too. Chase had welcomed him back with open arms. His brother let Max stay in his house and had given him a job. "Okay, when do you want me to start?"

Alex sighed heavily and dropped his head. "Thank you."

Max wasn't a touchy-feely kind of guy. Normally he did everything he could to avoid contact with others, but he found himself reaching over and patting Alex's shoulder. "Sure, I'm glad to help."

"I knew you would be," Chase said proudly.

Max warmed to his brother's praise.

"Chase can go over everything with you." Alex stood. "I need to get back to the house. Cassie is with Jacob right now, but he has to work today."

Max nodded and waited until Alex was out of the door before turning to his brother. "What else?"

Chase rubbed his hands roughly over his face. "Alpha Shawn is concerned about the publicity the gallery is getting. Several of the artists, Cassie in particular, have gotten a lot of attention. Last week we received a threat that if we didn't cancel the upcoming show, we would regret it. It was from the Church for Humanity, the people the wolves have had problems with ever since we went public. Our Pack didn't go public, and Shawn isn't sure how much longer he can hide us if the Church has targeted us."

"Is that really a big concern? From what I've seen, there have only been a few issues since the shifters announced their presence."

"It's a concern," Chase told him. "The Coalition between all the shifter species is brand-new. We're hoping that will protect all shifters, but until we know for sure, we still want to remain secret. Some of the human lawmakers are talking about forcing shifters to register."

"Register?"

"Yeah, so they can have a database on all of us."

"That's not right," Max said in disgust.

"I know. Shawn is talking with the council about what we can do, but he's worried."

"Well, I'll do what I can," Max promised.

"Good. How are you feeling?"

He knew his brother was concerned. Chase might not know everything that had gone down with his last mission, but his brother knew him well. Chase had also witnessed some of his nightmares.

"I'm fine."

Chase didn't look like he believed him but didn't push. "Scott's coming in. I thought we could grab your stuff, then I'll follow you over to the Wilson ranch."

"Sure." Max picked up the empty coffee cups. "Let me just finish cleaning up real quick."

"Okay, I have to grab a few things from the office, anyway."

Max went back into the kitchen to wash the last of the pans he'd used earlier. He didn't like leaving a mess. His brother might own the diner, but Max always pulled his weight. He hoped he would be an asset for the Wilson family. He remembered they had always been so happy. Very similar to his own. They'd never treated him any different either.

He was scrubbing the last pan when Scott Little walked in the back door.

"Hey, man!" Scott waved at him.

Max inclined his head since his hands were still in the water. "Thanks for coming."

"No problem," Scott assured him. "Didn't have anything planned today anyway."

Scott attended the community college in the next town over and was an okay kid. Max enjoyed their shifts together as well as Scott's quirky humor.

"You about ready?" Chase called from the front of the diner.

Max rinsed off the pan then placed it in the strainer. "Yeah."

He waved to Scott as he joined his brother out front. He grabbed his jacket and keys from under the counter. Together, they left.

One of his first purchases when he'd returned to the States had been his Harley. Chase had tried to get him to use one of the Alpha's many vehicles, but Max enjoyed riding the bike. He craved the freedom that the motorcycle provided him.

He'd found that the best time to ride down the canyon was just before sunset. The gorgeous views on the back of his Harley could not be seen the same way in a truck or an SUV. Max threw his leg over the bike and turned the key. The machine came alive under him. He couldn't suppress his grin. Yes, motorcycles were dangerous, and he loved every single second he was on his.

Chase waved at him as he climbed inside his truck.

Chase's house was just outside the city limits. He needed to be close to the Alpha in case any problems arose. The fifteen-minute ride was smooth and without a lot of traffic. Max's brother was ahead of him as they both drove in the same direction.

The Wilson ranch was farther inside the canyon lands. He would be able to take his bike there and hopefully would have time to ride some of the private roads. Plus, there was good hiking around the Wilson place. He didn't know if Cassie Wilson hiked, but he sure hoped so. It would be nice to be able to get some fresh air and just be away from everyone and everything.

He pulled up beside his brother's truck then turned the engine off. Chase's abode was small compared to a lot of the other Pack houses. But the three-bedroom structure was enough for them. Chase had welcomed the company when Max had come back to town. Their parents had offered to let Max stay with them. However, he was glad Chase had suggested they live together. He loved his mom and dad, but at forty, he didn't want to live with them again.

"I'm going to take a shower while you get your things together," Chase informed him.

Max nodded and made his way to his bedroom. He didn't have a lot. Just clothes and a few things he'd kept in storage. Even the furniture in the bedroom was his brother's.

Finally, Max felt like he was putting roots down. Eventually, he would buy his own home and concentrate on discovering what he wanted to do with the rest of his life. Whether he'd stay in Canyon or move on, he wasn't sure. He had time to decide.

He grabbed two duffels out of his closet then started to pack. He didn't know how long he would be needed at the Wilson ranch. It was better to have too much stuff than to have to leave Cassandra to go pick up what he needed.

He threw in jeans, T-shirts, boxers, socks and a light jacket. Back at his closet, he reached up to the top shelf and brought down the lock box. Max carried the box to the bed and sat.

It had been six months since he'd opened it.

He removed the keys from his pocket and carefully unlocked then lifted the lid. Inside was his favorite gun. A .45 Desert Eagle.

He ran his fingers over the stainless-steel barrel and sighed. He hadn't held a weapon in his hand since he'd left the Navy. He wasn't sure he would even be able to fire it again.

As he sat on the bed, he could still smell the smoke from the last gunfight. He hadn't been shooting his Desert Eagle that day. The M4 that he'd had on his shoulder had run out of ammo and Max had looked down in horror when he'd realized the entire team had used all the bullets they'd brought with them.

The house they'd been hiding in was small. Evan Cruise had lain at Max's feet, wounded and crying out in pain.

Deep down, he'd feared that was it. They were all going to die over in some godawful place and no one would know all they had wanted to do was rescue the captured aid workers.

The missions were classified and Max wondered if Evan's family would even be given his body.

The guerilla fighters who had gotten the jump on them had still been shooting into the house. Max had knelt beside his friend and gripped Evan's hand. He'd been in charge of his five-man team. It'd been up to him to get them out.

"You okay?"

Max started at Chase's voice. He slammed the lid closed on the gun box and stood. Quickly, he stuffed the container at the top of one of the duffels and faced his brother. "Yeah, just about done."

Concern was evident on Chase's face. Max had to ignore it. He wasn't ready to talk about what he'd been through. Actually, he couldn't speak to anyone about anything. He rushed into the bathroom then quickly packed everything he would need for the next several days.

When he returned to the bedroom, Chase was zipping up one of the bags. Max dumped his toiletries into the other then closed it. They each grabbed one as they headed out of the door. Max was relieved that Chase wasn't pushing him. He knew that he would have to share something with Chase soon. At the moment, his brother was giving him time.

"I'll take your bags over for you," Chase offered.

"Thanks." He passed the second duffel to his brother. Ready to go, he strode to the bike.

He could probably find the Wilson ranch on his own, but any time he had a flashback he was always a little shaky. He needed a few minutes to get his bearings, but he would have to follow Chase so he wouldn't get lost.

Chase backed out and Max waited until the dust settled, then followed. He was happy to have something to keep his thoughts off what he'd been through.

Hopefully this new job would help him clear his mind.

It took longer than he expected to reach the Wilson property. He slowed at the large gate where Chase was waiting. His brother waved him through and Max drove on. He pulled off to the side as Chase closed and locked the gate again.

Max was glad to see that they were indeed taking precautions on security.

Chase climbed back into his truck and started south. Max followed, using his senses to get familiar with the area. The main house loomed in the distance, a strong, solid structure that appeared inviting. Max could remember the barbecues that he and his family attended there when he was younger.

Even with the passing of their parents, it looked like the Wilson children had kept the property up. Green grass filled both sides of the paved road. As he pulled next to his brother and turned off his motorcycle, he could hear horses not far from him.

He turned his head to see if he could spot them and couldn't. He hadn't ridden in over a decade. His family didn't keep animals, and in the service, he hadn't had the opportunity. Excitement had him swinging off his bike. He'd always enjoyed the freedom of being on the back of one of the large animals. Luckily, even though the horses could sense the predator in a shifter, as long as a mount was treated with respect it didn't have any problems accepting shifters as riders or caregivers. The stallions and mares sure were trusting. In that regard, Max was envious of them.

"They still have horses?"

Chase nodded. "Yeah, Alex puts a lot of time into them."

"I thought he worked in the gallery."

Chase waved his hand. "He does. But his love will always be the horses first."

The front door opened and the subject of their conversation stepped out. "Hey, guys."

Smiling widely, Alex stomped down the stairs to greet them. He'd changed out of his slacks into jeans. Max was relieved to see Alex more relaxed, and glad he had agreed to help. It was great to be needed again.

They shook hands and Alex motioned toward the house. "Cassie's inside. Let's talk here before you go over to the house."

Max nodded and followed Alex and his brother.

The cool air hit him as soon as he walked inside. Max hadn't noticed just how hot he was until the air conditioning blew over him.

He must have made a sound, because Alex glanced back at him. "Cassie keeps the air on frigid. She can't stand being hot."

Since Max had spent way too much time in deserts and jungles, he agreed with her. "Feels good."

Alex grinned. "You'll fit in just fine."

He hung back, taking in the homey feel of the ranch house. The Wilsons had money, but he wasn't uncomfortable walking through the hall. The simple touches around the place were welcoming, not intimidating.

The hall opened into a large living room with beautiful wood flooring. Dark-brown leather couches dominated the space and a huge flat-screen television was placed over the stone hearth. In the corner, standing by the curved bar, was the most gorgeous woman he'd ever seen.

She smiled wide when their gazes met. "Wow! You grew up."

Max opened his mouth to respond then closed it again quickly. There was no way this sexy creature in front of him was Cassie Wilson. Gone were the braids and the crooked teeth. Instead, she had a pixie cut of short brown hair with streaks of blonde. She had to be only five foot five or so. She was tanned and had a body built for a man's hands. He had to clench his teeth to keep from reaching out for her.

He groaned mentally. Not what he had expected. Cassie Wilson was an attractive woman. Her soft chocolate eyes sparkled with amusement as she licked her lips.

Fuck! His cock hardened painfully. Max struggled to push aside his carnal needs and remember there were two other people in the room.

Chapter Two

Max's reaction shot a thrill through her. The way his gaze traveled up and down her body had Cassie holding back a shudder. Heat flushed into her face as his eyes lightened with arousal. His appraisal of her also gave her the opportunity to stare back at him. She'd suspected Max would be good-looking, since Chase and their dad were both attractive. Still, the hot, heavily muscled man across from her was *not* what she'd been expecting.

He was taller than both her brother and his, so that had to put him a few inches above six feet. His short black hair was a reminder that he'd just gotten out of the military. Wide hazel eyes stared into hers and his massive chest expanded with each breath. A tight black T-shirt, faded jeans and heavy boots made up his outfit. She wanted to see what was underneath those garments.

The tattoos covering both arms intrigued her. She wondered how he would respond if she ran her tongue along them—and wherever else he might have ink. *How much of him is covered in designs?*

She flushed and had to tear her gaze away from his body. She turned back to the mini fridge. "So...a beer?"

Alex chuckled and she wanted to sink into the floor. Of course her brother had caught her attraction to Max. There would be no living with him now. Alex was always trying to get her to step away from her studio and date. But until she'd gotten a look at Max, dating hadn't been a high priority. She'd grown up in a small town. Sure, she'd gone out with a few of the guys, but she had never been serious about any of them.

She popped the tops to four beers and strolled around the bar.

Max had settled on one of the couches and Alex and Chase took the one closer to her. She was going to have to take a seat next to Max. She glared at Alex, who merely grinned in response.

Her heart pounded as she moved farther into the middle of the room.

She passed the bottles to Chase and Alex, ignoring the gleam in her brother's gaze. She walked over and held out another beer to Max. Their fingers brushed as he took it from her and she barely held in a gasp at the electricity that sparked between them. A glance at his lap showed he was indeed as attracted to her as she was to him. The heavy aroma of arousal and need surrounded them. His erection pushed at the zipper of his jeans. A nice-sized package, she believed.

Since dropping to her knees to help him out wouldn't go over well with the other two men in the room, she backed away.

When she'd agreed to have Max hang around as security, she'd had no idea what she was getting herself into.

"Thank you."

His deep voice sent a thrill down her spine. Cassie managed a smile and nodded. She sat gently on the edge of the couch as Max took a long pull on his beer. She watched his throat work. Who knew a throat could be so damn sexy?

She caught herself staring and looked away. Her gaze passed over Alex, who was still smirking. She needed to get control over herself and stop fantasizing about what Max's large hands would feel like on her body.

Especially under the watchful attention of her brother.

"Shall we get started?" Alex asked in amusement.

She shrugged.

Alex, Chase and Max started going over the plan to beef up security on the property. Since she wasn't hearing anything that she objected to, she just listened. Listened and watched.

Max reclined back with the bottle held loosely between his fingers. He was a big guy but appeared comfortable. He had a certain amount of power surrounding him. The wolf inside her recognized it and wanted to present herself for him. The only other person she'd ever felt that kind of radiating dominance from was her Alpha.

The inner strength that she was picking up on could very well be why she was so attracted to him. Constantly surrounded by such domineering men, she had found herself more and more comfortable around the type, although her reaction to Max was different from how she'd responded to anyone else she'd ever met.

She studied her brother as his voice rose and fell in a calming manner. Alex was leaning forward, speaking directly to Max about the alarm system. She'd grown up in a loving home. Every day she had known she was loved and her parents had doted on each of their children. Alex had taken on the role after their parents' deaths in a car accident on an icy road. He'd just graduated from college and had returned to care for her and their younger brother, Jacob.

While he had a business degree and did in fact make a lot of money at the gallery, she knew that it was the ranch, the horses, that Alex truly loved.

The money that the family had, that Alex had made, always went to the animals first. Alex put everything he had, every free minute into the horses. Back when he'd first returned, Alex had been involved with a woman in college. Cassie had met her once, right after their parents' deaths.

She didn't know what had happened between Alex and the woman, but she'd never seen her again and Alex refused to talk about it.

Instead, Alex spent his time trying to get her to settle down like Jacob. So far Cassie had managed to turn the tables on him about settling down, but now she wasn't certain she wanted be able to anymore.

Chase picked up where Alex trailed off, getting into the security cameras and how more should be added. They only had cameras outside the house and stables. Chase wanted some installed in the interior of the buildings, too.

"I don't want cameras in my studio," Cassie spoke up.

The three men turned to her.

"The studio was the target," Chase responded. "It makes the most sense to cover that area."

Cassie shook her head. "No. I can't work knowing someone is watching me."

"They will only be there for your protection. It's not like we'll be watching them all the time," Alex assured her.

There was no way she could handle even that. "No, please."

Alex opened his mouth, but beside her, Max held up his hand. "Let's wait. We can go ahead and order some more cameras. If Cassie doesn't want them inside, we'll place them over the entry doors. We can work it out so everyone is comfortable."

Relief washed over her. She was glad Max seemed to understand. She nodded in acceptance.

"Let me look through the houses and I'll make a map of where I think the new cameras should go. I assume we'll do both the main house and Cassie's?"

"Jacob's, too," Alex added. "I want them covered."

Max inclined his head. "I agree."

Chase stood. "It seems like you all have everything under control. I need to stop back by the Alpha's place and make sure the new shifts in town have been sorted out. I'll update him on the situation here."

Alex and Max both rose with him.

"I expect you'll hear from the Alpha soon anyway. He'll want to check on things himself."

"I'll walk you out," Alex offered.

"If you're ready to take me over, I'd like to see the studio." Max turned to her.

Cassie placed her beer on the side table then wiped her hands down the legs of her jeans. Suddenly she was very nervous about having Max in her personal space. She spent the majority of her time in the studio. It was her heart and soul. Only a few people had ever been there.

"Yeah, sure." She climbed to her feet. "Uh, thanks, Chase. We'll see you later, Alex."

She waited while Chase hugged his brother and he followed Alex out before she turned to Max.

"Ready?"

He nodded.

She led the way out of the patio door and down the steps.

It was only a few yards from the main house's porch to the front of her place. Since the break-in, she had been better at locking and setting the alarm whenever she left.

Alex still hadn't forgiven her for forgetting the night before. But in all honesty, she'd never been the best at remembering. She'd never been worried about someone breaking in. They would have to get into the canyon, go through the property then get in and out without anyone seeing them. And why would anyone want to destroy her art, anyway?

All the questions that she just couldn't answer, no matter how much she thought about it, weren't really helping her not to worry, either.

She unlocked the front door with Max close behind her. Her hand shook slightly, but she didn't think he noticed.

After she pushed the door open, the long beep from the alarm alerted her that it was still armed. She punched in the four-number code and turned to face Max.

"Who has the code?"

"Me, Alex, Jacob and Peyton. Oh, and James."

"James?"

"He's been working as my assistant. He just graduated and is trying to get his own showing. He's very talented."

"How long has he been working for you?"

"About six months or so. He applied at the gallery and Alex hired him for the reception desk. We met and started talking, and he now works part-time for Alex and part-time for me."

"Last name?"

Cassie frowned at him. "James wasn't involved."

Max lifted an eyebrow.

"Strut. His last name is Strut."

"Is he part of the Pack?"

"No, he's not a shifter."

Max nodded, but Cassie couldn't let it go. "He's a good kid. There is no way he was involved." She needed to be heard. James had seen how hard she'd worked each and every day. He respected art and what she did.

The look Max sent her said he wasn't convinced. "Then he has nothing to worry about."

She sighed and figured he was right. She knew James was too dedicated to art for him to ever get involved in something like the break-in. In time, Max would realize he was off base suspecting him.

Max was glancing around and Cassie wondered what he saw. The entryway was open and painted a bright white. There were three wide archways that led farther into the residence.

"Through there is the kitchen." Cassie waved a hand. He would be able to see the stainless-steel appliances from where they stood. She pointed behind her.

"Living room and patio door." Then she faced the hallway opening. "Back here are the rooms."

He motioned for her to go ahead, so she stepped around him.

"The first door is the second bedroom," she told him as she turned the knob. The room was sparse with only a bed, dresser and nightstand. "This is where you'll be staying."

Max walked in and placed his two bags on the bed. He spun in a circle. "Okay, show me the rest."

Cassie didn't respond right away. It had just dawned on her that she would have a man staying in her house with her. A very attractive man who she wouldn't mind seeing naked. And he was just a couple of doors down from her bedroom.

When her palms started to sweat, she rubbed her hands down her thighs again.

Max's presence was a big deal in her life. He would see everything she was. There was no way she could hide her quirks from him.

"Cassie?"

She jumped, not realizing he had moved so close. She tilted her head back to look up at him. Damn, he was tall.

"It'll be all right," he assured her.

Cassie found herself shivering. She wanted to reach for him, have Max pull her into his arms. Have the press of his lips against hers. She swallowed and took a step back.

"Uh, I'm…uh…"

He smiled, his hazel eyes bright.

She was losing her mind. She whirled back around into the hallway and took several deep breaths to calm her racing heart.

"Okay," she said. "Next door is the bathroom. Then the office." She moved forward as she spoke. Then paused again. "My bedroom." The nervousness disappeared only to be replaced with dread when she stood in front of the last room.

She hadn't been back inside since she'd first discovered the incident. Cassie placed her hand on the wood. "The studio," she whispered. Her eyes burned with unshed tears. She couldn't do it…couldn't go in, not yet.

"Has it been cleaned up?" Max asked behind her. Just hearing his deep voice helped the nauseous pit in her stomach.

She nodded. "Alex took care of it. He said…"

Max's chest pressed into her back and he lifted his hand. "Deep breath," he spoke softly, his mouth close to her ear.

She inhaled through her nose then let the air out.

"Good," he said and opened the door.

In her mind, she could see the ripped canvases, the paint spilled over the floor and walls and her brushes in pieces. Cassie gasped in horror.

"It's all right," Max told her. "I'm right here with you. I won't let anyone hurt you again." Max held his hand down on her shoulder and she blinked.

None of that was there.

Alex had come through like always. The walls had been repainted the mint green that she'd had before. The hardwood floors were glistening and clean. The room had also been restocked.

Slowly, she stepped forward, one foot in front of the other. Her easels stood with blank sheets, her paints were lined up in their holders along the walls and her desk held a variety of brand-new brushes.

She made it to the middle of the room as tears fell from her eyes.

It looked good, but it also reminded her of what had been taken from her. Months of work ruined. She'd put her entire being into each piece. Now there was nothing to show for it.

Cassie sobbed. Max wrapped his arms around her.

"Shh," he cooed. "It will be okay."

Sure, she knew it could have been worse, but her heart ached. She clung to Max, allowing him to rock her gently. He felt good pressed to her body. As she soaked up the comfort he offered, peace filled her. Closing her eyes, she rested her cheek against his chest and just breathed in Max's spicy scent.

Her body started to respond. It was with regret that she forced herself to pull away. "I'm going to lie down for a little bit."

He released her. Their gazes locked, causing her breath to catch. His sparkling eyes were kind and called to both the woman and wolf inside her.

She spun on her heel, escaping into her bedroom. She had a lot to think about, because all signs were pointing to Max being more than just a bodyguard or security for her. The connection was so strong between the two of them that Cassie was unsure how she would let him go when everything was resolved. There'd never been another that made Cassie want to just curl up on his lap and relinquish control.

Cassie shuddered as she walked down the hall.

Could she give in to her desire and give Max what he was obviously offering? Yes, she thought she could. *But should I*, was the next question. She didn't even know Max as a man. Little pieces of gossip were not enough to tell Cassie what Max would truly want and need from her.

She sighed loudly once she was behind her closed bedroom door.

There was no denying she wanted him. Badly craved his hands and mouth on her. Her entire body tingled with need. How was she supposed to live in the same house with him and not give in? Hell, why would she even want to deny herself?

Yeah, she needed a nap, a hot shower and food. Then she could decide how to seduce Max Lawson into her bed, and hopefully, long term into her life.

* * * *

Max woke up with sweat pouring off him and his heart beating frantically. He had been back in that house, the room where he'd thought he was going to die, where his best friend hadn't made it out alive.

He clenched his eyes closed and tried to get control of himself and regulate his breathing. At least he hadn't woken himself up screaming. That would have probably scared the hell out of Cassie.

Even once his heart rate had slowed to almost normal, he wasn't able to get back to sleep, so he swung his legs over the side of the bed. A glance at the clock on the nightstand told him it was two in the morning. It had been so long since he'd gotten a full night's sleep. He should probably take one of the sleeping pills that the doctor had given him, but he didn't like how they made him feel the next day. Given his need to keep an eye out for Cassie and the Wilson family, he couldn't very well be stoned during the day.

Max pushed himself off the bed then pulled on the jeans from earlier. He would get a bottle of water from the kitchen and look over the plans for the Wilson ranch. He'd already gone over everything with Alex the night before, but another look wouldn't hurt.

He opened his bedroom door quietly, not wanting to wake Cassie, who slept only a few doors down. The fact that he could picture how sweet she'd look curled up in the middle of a large bed spoke volumes to how complicated this assignment was.

There was no doubt he'd been shocked when he'd seen her again. He wasn't sure why he'd still pictured the young girl from his memories, but Cassandra Wilson was in no way a little girl.

She was a beautiful woman.

It had thrown him off balance when she'd looked at him with those expressive chocolate-brown eyes. He hadn't been prepared for the punch he'd felt from the pixie woman.

She was much smaller than his big frame. And every single part of him had wanted to wrap her up and protect her.

It had just about killed him when they'd entered her studio and he'd seen the devastation on her face. Yes, the room had been cleaned, but he could see that she was picturing the way she'd found it before.

With her in his arms, he'd wanted to kill whoever had hurt her. His normally quiet and calm wolf had not been any happier. The itch under his skin had been an experience he had only felt a few times in his life. Since he couldn't shift into his animal, he could pretend it wasn't even there more often than not. But sometimes, when he was stressed or emotional, there was an extra awareness of his wolf.

Just as he'd started to wonder about his wolf's response to Cassie, she had shut down.

She'd excused herself from the room and told him she was tired. A door inside the studio apparently led to the bathroom that then connected to Cassie's bedroom.

Alex had shown up about thirty minutes after Cassie left him. When he asked about Cassie, Max explained what had happened. Alex had finished the tour and told him about the adjoining doors to Cassie's rooms.

While Alex went and checked on his sister, Max had started drawing a map of where he wanted the extra cameras installed.

Cassie's studio had a balcony door that linked to the sliding glass door of her bedroom. He'd made a note that both of those exits needed a camera above them. Cassie would still be able to open them when she wanted, but they would be able to see if anyone tried to enter that way.

He didn't turn on any lights until he reached the kitchen. There, he flicked on the switch and saw a half-empty bottle of wine on the marble counter. Cassie must have gotten up during the three hours he'd managed to sleep.

He pulled a cold bottle of water from the fridge and drank half of it down. He was starting to calm down and feel better already.

Thoughts of the woman replaced the aftershocks of the nightmare.

Since Cassie had been holed up in her room, he'd had a simple meal of a burger and some chips with Alex earlier in the night. He wished he could offer the family more reassurance, but he still didn't know what was going on.

The worry Alex had for his sister had been evident as they'd talked over dinner.

Max had vowed that he would get to the bottom of the break-in. And he would keep that promise. His laptop still sat on the island top. He checked the alarm and cameras Alex had given him access to. The blinking red light showed him that one of the balcony doors was open. He frowned. Surely Cassie wouldn't have forgotten to close up once she returned to bed. Not after what had just happened to her studio.

He grabbed his water and hurried down the hall. All the interior doors were still closed. Not wanting to go into Cassie's bedroom without invitation, he paused at the studio door.

He listened but couldn't hear any sound coming from inside.

Slowly, he turned the knob and, as silently as he could, pushed the door open. The first things he spotted were several large canvases tossed on the ground half-completed. One of the easels held a blank sheet and paint tubes lay scattered around on the wheeled table. She had made it inside and began working after all. Pride filled him. Cassie was a fighter and this just proved it.

He peered further into the room and spotted her.

She did, indeed, have the balcony doors open as she sat on the deck leaning against one of them.

Max stepped into the room. He hadn't expected to really find her there. He'd thought the worst. That another break-in had taken place and he'd failed her. His heart was still pounding with the flood of adrenaline.

Max wasn't sure if he should leave without being noticed or venture farther inside. He didn't want to disturb her.

"Couldn't sleep?" she asked quietly, not even turning her head.

"No," he replied. Since she'd spoken first, he decided to take a chance. He walked closer. "I see you started working."

She snorted. "It was all shit."

The anger in her tone surprised him. He strolled forward then paused in the doorway. She looked a little lost, holding an empty wine glass and staring out into the night.

"I'm sure it will take a bit to get back into the rhythm."

She shook her head. "Fucking sucks."

Max wondered if she was drunk. He crouched down beside her. "What?"

She turned her head to look at him.

He saw frustration in her eyes. "I can't reproduce what I lost, never have been able to. I paint…what I feel at the time. And right now I feel nothing, so all that" — she waved a hand back into the studio—"was just a waste of time."

Unable to offer much in words, Max decided just to listen to her talk. He didn't know much about art. However, even he had heard about Cassie's work. She'd been scared, but if he were honest, he preferred the fury. He stretched his legs out and mirrored her position against the second door. He knew what it felt like to have his entire world turned upside down. Sometimes a person just needed to vent. Max could offer her an ear at least.

"I wonder if they knew," she continued. "Whoever did this shit — did they know that I would never be able to make up what I lost?"

"I don't know."

"Yeah." She sighed. "I guess it doesn't matter, anyway."

When she didn't say anything else, he racked his brain on what he could do to help. "Tell me about your favorite painting."

Her eyebrows drew together. "Favorite?"

He nodded. "Yeah, out of everything you've ever done, what's your favorite?"

She smiled. "Jacob and Peyton's wedding present."

"Tell me about it."

"About six months before the wedding, Peyton and I went for a run. She was getting nervous about everything left to do for the wedding and I'd just finished my first showing and was exhausted."

She paused and looked at him. He inclined his head for her to continue.

"We drove farther into the canyon where no one else would be. We shifted and... God, I still remember it. It had been so long since I'd transformed into my wolf. The freedom... I remember thinking that if I never turned back it would be okay."

She laughed then. "But Peyton was still all tied up inside, so we ran. It must have been for hours. It was still early when we'd first started out and even when it got dark we didn't stop. We chased turkey and a few small critters, but we weren't after any of them. We just needed to let loose."

Max could see it. He could picture it perfectly as she shared her memory. He'd never experienced for himself what she spoke about. Although, listening to her, he felt closer to another shifter than he ever had in his life.

"Alex and Jacob must have gotten worried. They followed our trail and found us. I knew Alex was mad, so I shifted back. But Jacob just went over to Peyton and buried his muzzle into her neck."

Her voice softened. "It was then that I realized how much they really loved each other. Watching Jacob and Peyton together, I could feel my fingers wanting to reconstruct that moment. Alex and I left the two of them alone and I came straight here. I painted the two of them in a couple of days. Didn't eat, didn't sleep, I just had to get it down on a canvas."

Cassie met his gaze with tears in her eyes. "It was perfect. The moment that I saw, and I gave it to them. They both cried, they loved it so much."

Max wished he could see the painting she was talking about so passionately.

"That was my favorite."

Since she was smiling, he was glad he had asked.

The silence was comfortable as they relaxed for several long minutes.

"Can I ask you a question?" she said.

"Sure," he said easily.

"You don't have to answer if you don't want. I'm just curious."

He couldn't imagine anything that he wouldn't want to tell her. "Go ahead."

"You can't shift, right? Like at all?"

Surprised, Max jerked. Everyone in the pack knew he was a non-shifter. "No."

She pressed her lips together. "Sorry, I shouldn't have asked."

He hadn't meant to snap. "No, it's okay. It's just been a long time since anyone has brought it up."

She nodded but didn't look at him.

"Why do you ask?" He wasn't sure why he wanted to know but he couldn't see Cassie being cruel. There must have been a reason she was curious.

"I was sitting out here thinking," she said quietly. "I haven't shifted in a few weeks and was getting restless. I just wondered if you felt like that. If it bothered you?"

Max took a long drink, finishing his water. "It bothers me," he confessed.

Her head turned back to him.

"When you spoke about what it felt like... The freedom? I want to know that."

"I'm sorry," she started.

He held up a hand. "I always felt left out when the pack shifted together. At first, when I was young, one of my parents would have to stay with me. Then as I got older I could be left on my own. Don't get me wrong—everyone tried to include me, but it wasn't the same."

"That had to be terrible."

Grunting, he nodded.

"Is that why you left?"

No one had ever asked him that. He was sure his parents and Chase knew, even suspected Alpha Shawn had a good idea, but no one had ever said the words out loud. "Yes."

"But you can feel him? Your wolf?"

"Sometimes," he admitted. "I don't think it's the same as you or Chase, but there have been times I'm uneasy or the animal tries fighting to get out. I've dealt with him long enough that I can ignore it but..." He didn't really want to share how much he had despised his wolf at one time.

It sucked to be different. Growing up, he had just wanted to fit in.

They sat for a few more moments in silence.

"I bet he's fucking beautiful."

He'd been staring out into the dark night and jerked at her words. He turned to her. She was blushing, her fingers twined together, legs moving slightly.

"Yeah?" he asked, pleased.

She peeked up at him through her bangs and nodded.

"How would you describe him?" he questioned.

She bit her lip and searched his face. He didn't know what she was looking for, but whatever it was, she must have found it.

"Black, he would be pure black. Chase has some white and gray in his coat, but you would be solid black."

He was charmed by her. Wanting, maybe even needing more, he moved closer. "And?"

"Powerful." She scooted the few inches that separated them "Strong and dominant, but not pushy. He'd have broad shoulders and a wide chest."

He wasn't sure he should find the conversation about his inner animal so arousing, but it was. His cock was half-hard and getting fuller by the minute.

"A born leader." She spoke softly. "I'd follow you."

Their thighs were touching, and he was close enough to catch that her breathing had picked up. He turned his upper body toward hers as she angled her head back to look him in the eye.

"Anything else?" he asked as he raised his hand to her throat. He ran his thumb under her chin.

"Sexy, so damn sexy. Just like you are in human form."

There was no way he could have denied the attraction that was sparking between them. He slowly inched forward, keeping his gaze locked with hers. Cassie didn't back away. Their lips met with the slightest touch. He backed his head a little and watched her eyelids flutter then close.

She was the sexy one. He pressed their mouths together with more force and was rewarded with a moan from her. She gripped the back of his neck while their lips moved against one another.

He teased her bottom lip until she opened for him. Max threaded his fingers through Cassie's hair and held her head tightly, plundering her mouth. She arched into him, opening even more.

It had been so long since he had been with anyone and never had he felt this fierce so quickly. He wanted to claim and control her.

Cassie's fingers dug into his arms as she pushed into his hold. She wanted this just as badly as he did. It would be so easy to just roll on top of her and let them sate their hunger for passion.

But it was too soon. They still had a lot to learn about each other. He really was starting to believe that Cassie was the type of woman he'd always searched for. The mate he would find himself settling down with someday. First, he had to make sure he would be able to take care of whomever he chose to mate with. He'd somehow lost himself along the way and he needed to get back the man he'd once been.

He pulled back slowly and with regret.

She was still reeling from the events of the night before and he wasn't exactly a catch with his current emotional mess.

But it was so hard to back away when she stared up at him with need written clearly across her face.

"We shouldn't do this," he said to her.

She frowned but loosened her hold.

"We have time. We don't have to rush into anything." He barely got the words out before he was on his feet and stalking away. He had to put some distance between them. He was not strong enough to resist Cassie Wilson. If he didn't get away, he would end up claiming her for his own. And she had no idea who he really was.

Max closed his bedroom door firmly and leaned against the cool wood. For the second time in a day, he'd felt his wolf inside clawing to get out. He knew it was impossible, although if he could shift, he had no doubt he would be on four furry paws.

Running his palm over his heart, he closed his eyes — not that it would help. He could picture Cassie's desire then her confusion. He had screwed up royally.

He slammed his hand on the door.

It wouldn't be fair to Cassie to start something. He was still trying to deal with what had happened to him and his team. He grabbed the bottom of his shirt and whipped it over his head. Then, with determination, he walked to the mirror above the dresser.

He ran his shaking finger lightly around the tattoo over his heart.

A name and date scrawled in black. The day that he'd lost his best friend in that hellhole.

Not being able to stop the dreams, unable to understand what had gone wrong, he wasn't able to offer himself to Cassie. He couldn't give her what he wasn't sure still existed.

Chapter Three

Max managed to fall back asleep, but it hadn't been easy. In addition to being trapped in that rundown house with his team, now the dream had Cassie there as well.

He had been trying to protect her right as the explosion had gone off.

Then he woke up.

Max's nightmares were getting worse and if he didn't get them under control, he wouldn't be any help to Cassie or her family. The Pack meant the world to him and Max didn't want to fail them.

Sweating and shaking, he stumbled to the bathroom to try to wash the dream away. The other doors in the hall were all closed, so he didn't know if Cassie was awake yet.

His head might not be on straight about relationships, but he would make sure that Cassie was safe so they would be able to explore the strong connection between them. Lying in bed the night before with her scent still surrounding him, he'd been happy for the first time in longer than he could remember.

Max just needed to get his shit together. The sticky sweat made him feel gross and dirty so he needed a quick clean up. That would help clear his thoughts as well. He turned the shower knob on hot and closed the door to warm up the glass stall. He bent over to the sink to peer at himself in the mirror.

The dark circles that he had been carrying around the last couple of months were worse. His skin was too pale, plus the weight loss he'd suffered was more obvious.

He needed to take better care of himself. He couldn't figure out why Cassie would even be attracted to him in his current state. But there was something about her. Whenever they were in the same room, he felt a pull in her direction.

There were some decisions that he needed to make. He didn't like the person he was becoming. Now, if he could just figure out how to get back everything he'd lost in himself, he would have something to offer Cassie. He needed to be his own man again.

Determination pulsing inside him, he pushed away from his image and climbed into the shower. The almost scorching water pelted down on him and he sighed deeply as his muscles relaxed.

He grabbed the shower gel off the shelf and poured a good amount into his palm. With his other hand, he used a washcloth to scrub himself clean. He felt better and the fog from the nightmare lifted.

Max rolled his shoulders and rinsed the soap from his body before shampooing his hair. Keeping the buzz cut from his Navy days saved him time.

Body freshened up, he fisted his half-hard cock, sliding his hand slowly up and down. He'd been somewhat hard since he'd first laid eyes on Cassie. After he'd returned to the States, he'd had had his hand for company. And that was when he could even get it up. But all of that was changing.

He tightened his hold and, stroking himself faster, called up the memory of the kisses they'd shared the night before. Cassie's soft lips beneath his played through his mind and the pressure of her body heightened his arousal.

He groaned and his cum squirted, painting the shower wall. It had been a long time since he'd gone over the edge so quickly. With a lighter air, he rinsed once more, making sure to clean the wall, then turned the water off. He grabbed one of the towels from the rod next to him and dried himself just as a knock came from the front of the house.

Max wrapped the cloth around his hips and rushed to his room. He pulled on a clean pair of jeans before grabbing a short-sleeved T-shirt. He dragged the top on as he headed toward the front entrance.

"Coming!" he called when the knock came again.

Just as he reached for the handle, he caught the scent of his Alpha outside. Max took a deep breath and opened the door. He'd been expecting his Alpha to show up at any time. In fact, Shawn had been too good at giving him space, so Max knew he'd been caught.

Alpha Shawn stood on the porch holding a takeout container with three cups and a bakery bag. He held them up in offering.

Max grinned and waved the man inside. "Hey."

"Max, I hope I'm not disturbing you."

"Of course not. Please come in."

Alpha Shawn walked through the entry and into the kitchen. Max followed behind, both pleased to see his Alpha again and nervous at the same time. Alpha Shawn had a way of making Max confess things he would rather keep hidden. He'd been doing his best to avoid his Alpha since he'd returned home.

It figured that as soon as he was starting to pull his head out of his ass, he'd no longer be able to steer clear of Alpha Shawn. While his Alpha set the coffees on the island countertop between them, Max walked to the cabinet to pull out some plates.

"I don't know if Cassie is awake yet, but I can check."

Alpha Shawn shook his head. "No, it's okay. I'd like a few minutes with you anyway."

Max nodded. His Alpha didn't just stop by for no reason. Everyone in the Pack knew that their leader was always looking out for them. Even Max knew that he could only hide for so long.

"So how are you doing?"

"I'm fine," he assured his Alpha.

Shawn leaned against the counter and lifted an eyebrow. "You sleeping okay?"

"Sure," he lied. Of course, his Alpha could smell the scent of deception so Max clarified his statement. "Some nights are better than others, but I'm handling everything."

Instead of calling him on his lie, Shawn just shook his head. "I have no doubt that you're handling everything, but that doesn't mean you can't ask for help if you need it. It takes a strong man to lean on others."

He sighed. "I know… I just need to figure things out." There was no use pretending. His Alpha had that stoic look on his face whenever he was determined to get through to one of the Pack members. "I just need more time."

"Okay." Shawn smiled. "I won't push right now. You know you can always talk to me, don't you?"

"Of course."

"All right." Shawn lifted the lid off one of the cups and Max followed suit. The smell of the fresh coffee was perfect and his stomach growled. "I brought some muffins, too."

"Thanks." He dug into the bag and chose one of the banana-nut muffins. He bit into it and moaned. *God, these are so damn good.*

"How are things going here?"

He chewed and took a long sip of his coffee. Alpha Shawn wouldn't know what had taken place between him and Cassie the night before, but Max still found himself shifting his feet nervously. "I…uh…well…we…"

"Max?"

As he took another drink, he mentally cursed himself. "Everything is okay. I've only just really started. I have some ideas on how to increase security and add a few more cameras without being too intrusive."

"Good, good. After this mess is over, I hope to talk to you about the rest of the Pack."

That sounded like his Alpha wanted more than just a favor. "Well, you know that I'm happy to help in any way that I can, but I'm not a security expert or anything. Don't you have people for that?"

"Yes, but they're not Pack. I want someone who I can trust to oversee them. This incident has shown me that we've been lucky so far. A lot of other Packs have had direct attacks against them. I want to prepare before that happens here. That's where you come in."

"You want me to do it? To oversee security for the Pack?" Max asked in disbelief. That was a major responsibility. He wanted to contribute to his community, but he wasn't sure he could handle such a large job.

"Absolutely."

"I'm not sure I'm the right person," he said honestly. He couldn't even sleep all the way through the night. His Alpha didn't know everything that was going on in his head. If he did, there was no way Shawn would want him.

"You're the perfect person. You're a strong leader, smart, dedicated, loyal and compassionate."

He blushed at the compliments. Even though he knew he wasn't those things, at least not anymore. "I'm not sure."

"It's something that I want you to think about. Take care of things here and see if you can find out who broke into Cassie's studio, then make sure your sole focus is to protect her. The rest will work itself out."

He sure as hell hoped so. He nodded.

"I knew I could depend on you." Shawn patted his back as he passed Max. "I'll show myself out. I want to stop by and have a quick word with Alex while I'm here."

Max stood speechless as Shawn did, in fact, leave on his own. He wanted to be polite and at least walk the man to the door, but he couldn't seem to make his feet work. His Alpha's words were still bouncing around in his head. Shawn believed in him. He wished he was as sure as his Alpha. Before his last mission had gone to shit, he'd had the confidence that Shawn was showing in him. He'd even been a little bit cocky. It was weird how one day could change all of that.

All he'd ever wanted to do was make a difference. To help people. When he'd left Canyon, he'd been a young man determined to show the world what he'd been made of. He'd joined the Navy and had known just weeks into boot camp that he'd found the place he was meant to be at.

He thrived at the physical part of training. He enjoyed pushing his body to its limits. The brothers he'd connected with were like an extension of his Pack. He'd been overseas and still thought he would spend his entire life in the service.

Eight years after he'd first joined, he'd applied to the Special Forces Units. It had taken everything he had to make it mentally and physically. Even so, he had never felt better in his life. The first missions had been simple gathering of intel. He hadn't really been in danger. Then he'd been transferred to his new team and everything had changed.

Under the cover of night, he'd found himself in some very fucked-up situations. Still, every time he'd made it back home, he'd been proud. When he'd been promoted and given his own squad, he'd vowed to bring each member home with him every time.

In the end, he hadn't been able to keep that promise to his fellow soldiers. He might have brought Evan's body back, but it had been under his command that the man had died.

He closed his eyes, fighting the memories, but they still bombarded him.

They'd dropped inside the enemy lines in the pitch blackness of night. The coordinates that they'd been given had just been a rough estimate. It hadn't been known whether the hostages were dead or alive.

But they'd had to try. *That's what we did.*

He'd led his small band of men deep into the jungle to complete their task.

It had been sickeningly hot, the air so thick it had been hard to breathe. Sounds they'd only heard a few times had followed them as they'd traveled farther and farther into danger.

Even when their boots had first hit the ground, he hadn't felt good about the mission. Something, some small part of him, had known there was just something off. He'd ignored the feeling and followed orders. He would always regret that.

They'd walked for two hours before they'd started to hear signs of life from humans instead of just the jungle animals. Max had stopped his team's forward movement with a fist in the air. He'd been well known for his above-average hearing. No one had known he was a shifter. They'd just teased him that it was his gut instinct, but they'd always followed him. Max had let them believe that.

* * * *

Max took point and methodically moved his men into position. They were just south of a small group of tents. One old, beat-up Jeep was parked to the side and it was filled with guns and ammo. They would need to secure that vehicle first. But that was a sure sign that the rebels were very well armed.

A few rough-looking men sat around a fire smoking and talking. He motioned to his team to drop and wait.

One by one their targets went into one of the sleeping areas. A large tent on the far side looked like their best bet for where to find the hostages.

He crawled over to Evan and the youngest member, Jon Banks. He gave the hand signal for them to approach and, after receiving nods of affirmation, he crept back, retaking his position.

Waiting until all was calm, he blew out a breath and sent his unit in.

Jose Sanchez guarded the vehicle while he and Matt Wallace covered Evan and Banks.

The shouts from the large tent alerted not only his team but also the enemy.

All hell broke loose, but Max had a clear view of the hostages running with Evan and Banks, so he motioned Sanchez to set the explosive and take out the extra guns and ammo. There wasn't enough time to secure the weapons on the bodies, but they needed to ensure that they couldn't be turned against them.

He and Wallace used their own rifles in the firefight and before he knew it, the huge explosion rocked the night.

"Move! Move!" he screamed. Max kept close, bringing up the rear as they disappeared into the darkness.

* * * *

If only things had ended there.

Max shook himself out of his thoughts. He knew he had to let go of what had happened. It wasn't easy. He relived that day over and over. His stomach was in knots as he pushed himself away from the counter. The first part of their mission had been a success. The rest had been one fuck-up after another. He had to keep busy to prevent himself from thinking about where things had gone wrong.

He picked up the extra coffee Alpha Shawn had brought then started down the hall.

If Cassie was awake, he'd give it to her. If not, he would check to make sure everything was secure.

He tapped softly on her studio door, hoping if she wasn't awake he wouldn't bother her. He heard movement in the room and cracked the door.

The patio door was closed and the room was much the same as it had been the night before. Except for one thing.

Sitting in the middle of the room on the easel was a painting. It wasn't one of the half-finished pieces he'd seen earlier. No, this was amazing...just amazing.

He pushed the door all the way open so he could get a better look.

He recognized the canyon cliffs of their home. The colors blended together so seamlessly it was almost like he could reach out and stroke the hard ridges.

Standing strong and powerful in the center of the canvas was a huge black wolf.

He nearly dropped the Styrofoam cup as he felt compelled to get closer.

It was the most astounding thing he'd ever seen. Inside his body, his wolf stretched in need. He hadn't been lying when he'd told Cassie he sensed the animal inside. But it was like she'd been able to peer deep inside him and paint how he pictured his wolf.

"Do you like it?"

He heard Cassie behind him yet couldn't look away from the wolf staring back at him. He even recognized the gaze that met his in the mirror. "Yes."

She moved closer, bringing the heat from her body next to his.

"After you left, all I could think about was showing you my vision. It was like I could see him and I wanted you to be able view your wolf through my eyes," she said quietly.

Max nodded. "It's remarkable." He turned suddenly and grabbed her to yank her forward. He slammed his mouth down on hers and kissed her hungrily.

Cassie had been so nervous about showing her newest piece to Max. She hadn't expected such a passionate response when he did see it, even though she'd felt exactly the same way. Cassie found herself pressed to Max as he ravaged her mouth. *God, it feels so freaking fantastic.* She'd never experienced such an overwhelming need for another person as she did with Max.

She gripped his shirt with her fists to keep him from stopping. They'd touched on some sensitive subjects earlier, but she knew there was more going on with him than his non-shifter status. Cassie wanted to know everything that made him tick. She'd realized that the night before. Max was everything she had always desired in a mate. They weren't ready to declare their love for each another, but she thought they might get there one day. There was a pull between them. And she needed him more every minute she spent with him.

He had one arm around her waist, anchoring her, but she wanted his full body, not just his mouth. She drew her lips back and looked down. His free hand still held a to-go cup.

He noticed her gaze. "Coffee."

Nodding, she took the cup from him then placed it on the shelf behind her. "Now," she said, framing his face with her hands. "Let's do that again."

She was the one to kiss him this time. He didn't hesitate to get right back to where they'd left off. Their mouths were fused together as Cassie rubbed against him.

He moaned and she swallowed the sound. He tasted so damn wonderful. Like coffee and something banana with just a hint of a spice. She could lose herself in his flavor and wouldn't regret it at all.

He pulled at the hem of her T-shirt until he managed to get it hiked up. At the first touch of his rough palms on her stomach, she began whimpering.

"Oh, hell," he panted against her lips. "You feel so good."

"Yeah." She leaned harder into him.

The doorbell rang. They froze. She stared into his gaze as saw the same frustration at being interrupted.

"Maybe they'll go away," she said hopefully. She didn't want to stop. Yes, they probably weren't ready to just fall in bed together, but the attraction between the two of them sizzled.

Max started to step away from her and she tried to hide her disappointment.

"It's probably for the best," he replied. "I need to check in with Alex about the additional cameras and look for weak spots. There's a lot of work to do."

She understood that he had a job there. However, it didn't stop her from almost obsessing about having his hands on her.

Cassie tugged her shirt back down then smoothed the material just as she heard the front door open.

"Cassie?"

"In the studio," she called out. "That's James, my assistant. He has a key," she explained to Max.

He nodded. He turned to walk away but paused at the painting again. "That is truly beautiful."

"Thank you."

James knocked on the open door and stuck his head in. "Hey."

"Hi." She waved him forward. "James this is Max, who is here as security. Max, my assistant, James."

"Security?" James looked between the two of them.

"After the break-in, Alex thought we needed to be more careful. Max is going to help get the house and studio better covered and is staying until the person is caught."

"Wow!" James stuck his hands in his pockets.

He was young, and a very talented artist himself. They'd met at the gallery and she had been taken with his enthusiasm for art.

"I didn't realize it was such a big deal."

Cassie frowned. "Of course, it is. Someone broke into my home and the studio. Months of work was destroyed!"

James nodded. "Yeah, it's just, no one was hurt and Canyon is usually such a safe place."

"I'm here to make sure it stays that way," Max said.

He was watching James closely. She knew that Max had to be suspicious of everyone who had access to the studio, but there was no way she would believe that James had been involved.

"I guess I was just hoping it was a mistake or something. It's scary."

"It'll be okay, hon," she assured him, wrapping an arm around his shoulders.

His bleached, spiked hair tickled her cheek when she embraced him.

"Wow!" James noticed the canvas of the black wolf and broke away. "This is so awesome!"

She met Max's gaze and smiled. She thought the man was pretty awesome himself.

"I'm going to get started," Max stated, "so don't leave the house without letting me know."

"No problem," she assured Max. "We're going to go through the inventory list from the gallery to see just how many more pieces I need. I don't want Alex to cancel the show if he doesn't have to."

Max's hand brushed against hers as he strolled from the room. The tingle that followed his touch gave Cassie something to look forward to.

"This is going to sell for sure," James said.

"No!" she exclaimed, a little too loud. "I'm not selling that one."

"What? Why not?" James asked. "It's even better than what you had originally painted."

The hours she'd spent didn't matter. There was only one person who she wanted to get to see the canvas every single day. Her creation, was for Max. "I'm not selling it."

"Okay," James said with a long sigh. "What do we need to do?"

Cassie looked around. "Let's decide how many more canvases we need."

"So, the show must go on?" James said.

Cassie looked at the painting she'd spent the night doing. At least her muse had returned. Her fingers itched. She could feel the urge to keep going. There were times when she was so motivated that she didn't do anything but work. It felt like this was one of those times.

Max turned the screw to secure the last additional camera Alex had purchased and sighed with relief. He'd been at it for hours. He was finally comfortable about the new security around the entire Wilson ranch. Cassie would be safe no matter what.

"Hey, man."

Max looked over at Alex, who had joined him on the porch. The man held out a beer and Max almost moaned in gratitude. It was damn hot out today and he was tired. He climbed down from the stool he was using for mounting the camera above the front door and accepted the cold bottle.

He rubbed it over his forehead before taking a long pull. "Thanks, I needed that."

Alex nodded as he glanced around. Max didn't miss the relief in Alex's eyes. Alex was really worried about his sister. "Looks like you got the last one up."

"Yeah, I also put new locks on all the windows and installed a chain on the front door. Cassie seems to use the balcony doors a lot and I want to get some better locks for that."

"Cassie likes to smell the fresh air," Alex said. "It's a habit I don't see her breaking."

Max noted that Alex seemed a little uneasy. He took another long drink and lifted an eyebrow. "Everything okay?"

Alex shook his head. "Let's sit."

Max followed him to the wooden porch chairs then settled down with his beer. "What's up?"

"You've heard about the Church for Humanity?"

Max didn't even want to think about where this was going. "Sure, they're the ones who're trying to get the government to make shifters register."

"They're also the reason that the wolf Council worked so hard in setting up the new shifter Coalition. The main guy was arrested in Nevada for kidnapping and all sorts of other crimes against the wolves came out."

"I remember reading about it right after I got home," Max told him.

"I received another letter today at the gallery that they want the showing canceled due to the *nature* of the show pieces."

"Cassie's work?" Max guessed.

Alex leaned forward and rubbed his hand over his face. "Yeah. I called and left a message for Alpha Shawn, but he hasn't gotten back to me yet. I'm worried. I know our Pack isn't public, but the Church can cause us all kinds of trouble."

"Do you think they might be responsible for the break-in?"

Alex blew out a breath. "I don't know. I mean, how would they have known we weren't home?"

"Someone was watching. Or it's someone close to Cassie or even you."

"And if someone is watching, what else have they seen? We shift all the time. Almost everyone around these parts does."

Max could completely see why Alex was worried. The members of the Church had been getting more and more vocal about how unnatural the shifters were. After their leader had been convicted, it had seemed to spread, turning downright nasty between the Church and shifter communities. "We need to call the Council."

"That's why I wanted to talk to Shawn. He'll be able to contact them and maybe even the Coalition."

"Fuck!" Max muttered. This just got worse every minute. If they did have to bring the Coalition in, there was no way they would be able to remain hidden. "What are we going to tell Cassie?"

"I don't know. I'm not sure we should tell her anything right now. She needs to concentrate on the upcoming show and I don't want her more worried than she already is."

"Then maybe you shouldn't discuss it on my front porch."

Max jerked his head to the side and saw Cassie standing in the doorway. Alex groaned and stood.

"I'm sorry, Cass, but I didn't want to scare you." Alex held out his hand.

Cassie moved to him and snuggled into his arms. "I'm a big girl, Alex. You can't protect me from everything." She looked over at Max. "Plus I've got a pretty good bodyguard."

Max grinned, although he fought not to blush. He really admired how calmly Cassie seemed to be handling everything. Yes, she was struggling, but her natural instincts seemed to take over and she showed trust in the men around her.

Alex chuckled and patted her back. She stepped away then leaned against the rail while Alex retook his chair.

"You can't keep things from me, Alex. If there is more going on than just a break-in, I need to know."

Alex nodded. "I know, you're right."

"We'll handle this," she told him. "But what about the boys? Are they safe here?"

"I sure hope so," Alex said just as his cell phone rang. He dug it out of his pocket. "That's Shawn. I need to take this."

Max waved him off and waited until he'd walked down the porch steps. He then turned his attention to Cassie. "You okay?"

"Yeah. No. I don't know," she said, sighing deeply. "I can't help but wonder if I caused all this with my paintings? Is the Pack in danger because of me?" It was her eyes that drew him in. Cassie was more than worried—she was scared. Max didn't know how to take the burden from her.

Max stood and encircled her in his arms. "No, I don't believe so. These people are so hell-bent on causing trouble for us they could have found anything." It was true. Max had always felt out of place. Like he didn't belong with the shifters but wasn't human, either. Now, seeing everything that had taken place while he'd been serving his country, Max questioned what he'd been protecting. Was it worth everything he'd sacrificed when humans were hell-bent on destroying his family? Max knew not all humans were hateful or dangerous, but he still wrestled with the decisions he'd made.

She laid her head against his chest. "I hate the idea of someone watching us. Planning ways to hurt us. I don't understand why they can't just let us be."

Max buried his hand in her hair and tightened his embrace. "Ever since the beginning of time, people have feared what they don't understand. This will pass. We have the Council and now the Coalition. It's going to be okay." He had to believe the words he spoke. He'd heard them time and again from his first Commander. Commander Gunther had been a shifter and had sniffed Max out during his first deployment. He was also the officer responsible for Max's transfer to special units. There had been nights when Max hadn't been able to sleep and he'd repeated the wise words that Commander Gunther had shared.

Max was proud he could talk about some of his time in the service with Cassie. He hoped the teaching could give her the comfort it had him on the many lonely nights out in the desert.

"I'm glad you're here. Everything is crazy and happening fast, but I feel safe with you. Like I can get back to my art and not worry about what is going on around me."

"I'm glad I can give you that kind of security," he replied. It was funny that from the moment he'd set eyes on Cassie, he had felt something settle deep inside him. Like even his wolf was at home with this woman. "And we'll figure out what to do about the Church."

Her eyes sparkled as she gazed up at him. "Kiss me again?"

He cupped her cheek while he lowered his head. "Yes," he whispered against her lips, brushing his over hers.

She pushed into the kiss eagerly and responded so beautifully that he had to draw back so he didn't end up embarrassing them both. Her brother might return at any time.

"Be good," he warned playfully when she tried to chase his mouth.

She lifted an eyebrow. "Oh, I can be so very good."

He snorted, stepping back. "Not with your brother close by," he teased, popping her on the ass with a light slap.

Her carefree laughter warmed his heart. They might have a lot of concerns, but they would get through them. He would make damn sure.

Max spotted Alex heading back toward them and retook his seat. Cassie smirked at him and returned to lean against the rail.

"Shawn is calling the Council right now. He and Chase will come over to the house as soon as they can," Alex informed them as he stepped up to the porch. "I'm going to call Jacob and make sure he can make it, too. I thought we could have a barbecue. It's a nice evening and we need some sort of routine."

Max glanced at Cassie to make sure she was up to spending time with her family. He wanted her to return to a routine and he was certain he had her house covered with as much security as needed. No one would be getting inside without him knowing.

"Sounds good," Cassie agreed. Max nodded. "I'll make a few side dishes. The least we can do is feed everyone if we're going to put them in danger," Cassie said.

"Hey!" Alex strode up the steps and to his sister. "This is not your fault."

"I know," she said softly. "Really, I do, but I can't help but... This sucks!"

Alex nodded as he chuckled. "It does. Just remember there are five artists in the showing. Four of them are shifters, and we don't even know why this show is being targeted. We've had many over the years. Let us figure this out."

She nodded. "I'm going to go start on some food."

Max kept himself from reaching out to her as she passed. He wanted to comfort her, to take her back to the moment when she was laughing happily. As she stepped back inside, Alex growled. Max turned to him.

Alex stood, hands fisted at his side. "I want to kill whoever is doing this to her, to us all."

Since Max felt the same way, he couldn't really offer an argument.

"I've got to call Jacob. Stay close to her?"

"I will," Max promised. He waited until Alex was stalking back to the main house, then turned and followed Cassie.

He found her at the kitchen sink, scrubbing potatoes. "You okay?"

"Fine," she answered shortly.

He moved up behind her and placed his hands on her hips.

She sighed and leaned back into him. "I forgot for a minute outside. With you. How can I be happy and so scared at the same time?"

Max nuzzled her neck. "It's natural. You've got a lot thrown at you right now. It's okay to feel good while you're still worried. It's okay to feel pleasure."

She faced him. "I just keep thinking, if all of this wasn't happening, I wouldn't have met you again. You wouldn't be here with me."

Max leaned closer and rubbed his nose against hers. "I think we would have. Somehow, we would have found each other. This, between us, is too good for us not to have found a way to each other. "

"Max," she whispered. "Kiss me."

Max did as she requested. He could spend forever kissing her. Sure, Max could be hiding in the back of his brother's café, keeping himself from the Pack, but seeing Cassie would have pulled him out into the open. He believed that. The connection between them was just too strong for them to ignore it.

He wasn't a catch. He had nothing to offer her. Hell, he didn't even have his own place. But none of that seemed to matter when she fit so perfectly in his arms. When her body against his made him feel alive.

With Cassie, Max didn't feel like a failure. He was invisible and anyone who wanted to hurt her would have to go through him.

Chapter Four

Cassie felt better. She'd made potato salad, dips for chips and coleslaw for dinner, then she'd stepped into a quick, hot shower. Max hadn't even tried to join her and she was a little disappointed. She kept telling herself that they'd have time together, but she was struggling with patience. She wanted the man.

While she'd cleaned up, Max had linked all the new cameras from her place, the main house and Jacob's residence to his laptop. He'd taught her how to work the programs and she appreciated that he was including her, showing her how he was keeping her safe.

He had the laptop on the deck table as they waited for everyone to arrive. Alex had started the grill before pulling beers out of the cooler and passing them around.

There was a nice cool breeze that Cassie welcomed as she sat next to Max, admiring him. With his head bent over the computer screen, she was able to watch him without him noticing. He was so damn attractive with his black hair and tan muscular body. She could still feel his hands on her from earlier in the kitchen and arousal shot through her.

Max lifted his head and looked over at her. Catching her staring at him, he winked. "Later," he murmured.

She ducked her chin, lifting her gaze to Alex, and flushed when she realized her brother had been watching her while her attention had been on Max. Alex was grinning at her, but luckily she heard footsteps. She turned to see Alpha Shawn and Chase arriving.

Max pushed the laptop away and stood. He greeted his brother with a quick hug then shook hands with their Alpha. She liked the way his hazel eyes brightened around the other men. He stood next to Chase and Cassie could easily see how close the two brothers were. That was important to her. It had just been her and her siblings for so long. Both Alex and Jacob made it a point to take care of her while she did her best to return the favor. She didn't like to leave the ranch, so they did her shopping and visited a lot. While there was no getting out of gallery shows, one of them stayed with her the entire time.

Alex had even been the one who had hired James for her. He'd wanted the young artist to get more attention and had asked Cassie to help him. Since she and James had hit it off right away, she was happy to assist in his training.

James didn't have a lot of money, so the income that came from helping Cassie provided him with some cash, while, at the same time, the experience of working with another artist had really brought James' art to the front.

There would be half a dozen of James' works in the next showing, which was one reason why she didn't want it to be postponed. This was really James' true first shot.

Since he was human, he wouldn't be at the barbecue, but she had spoken to him earlier about what was happening. She had assured James that the show would still proceed as planned. His art would be seen.

James had been relieved. Since he didn't know about the shifter aspect of the break-in, he had been more upset that someone was trying to hurt the gallery, stop the showing from being held.

She wished she could be honest with him. Since her Pack wasn't in the open, she had to continue to be careful. Even if she trusted James, Cassie couldn't make the decision to share the secret that belonged to everyone in the Pack.

Just one more thing she had to keep from her assistant.

"What are you thinking about so hard?" Max asked as he slid to her side.

"The show. I told James it would still go on. It's his first art exhibition and I want to make sure that he has enough support. He doesn't know about shifters so this entire situation is really upsetting to him."

"How long has he worked for you?"

"About six months I believe, Alex would know for sure. He applied for the job over the internet and moved up here. He doesn't have any family so he became part of ours. Plus, he's a big help. I don't have to worry about ordering supplies or anything else other than painting."

"He seems kind of young."

"Yeah, but he is talented. A few more years and he'll probably have a show of his own." She nudged his hip. "You're looking into him?"

"I am," Max admitted. "He has access to the ranch and knows all of you."

"There's no way he's involved." Cassie knew deep down that James was a harmless human and nothing more.

"Then he has nothing to worry about. Let me do my job, Cassie. He won't even know I'm looking if he doesn't have anything to do with this."

She had to trust Max, though she disagreed. If they were going to be able to explore the attraction between the two of them, she'd have to take Max at his word. There was a reason that she responded so strongly to him. "Just be careful. He's been through a lot."

"I will." He squeezed her shoulder before moving over to the grill.

"I take it everything is working out between you and Max?" Alpha Shawn asked as he took Max's place at her side.

She grinned over at him. "Did you have any doubt?" Her Alpha might be the strong, silent type, but he knew what he was doing. Putting Max with her had to be more than just protecting her. She didn't know Shawn's angle, but he'd have one.

Shawn chuckled. "Nope." He swung his arm over her shoulder and led her away from the others. "I knew Max would be a big help here. And I was sure that you would be a good influence on him as well."

Cassie checked over her shoulder to make sure no one else was within hearing range. "Tell me you're not playing matchmaker." Not that she truly minded, but having her Alpha involved in her love life was weird.

"No, actually, I'm not," he assured her. "But Max needs to do something that will make him feel good about himself again, make him feel needed. I'd only trust him with a few select people. Your family is one of the best I've ever known. He needs time to heal and less time to think."

She tipped her head back to get a good look at him. "You're worried about him?" That was interesting. Even though she knew Max was hiding pain, she could see he wanted to fight through it.

"Yes," Shawn admitted. "I have plans for Max, but he needs to settle things in his mind before I can proceed."

"What kind of plans?"

"The kind I'm sure he'll fight me on. I want to name him as my successor if anything happens to me."

She couldn't hold in her gasp. "That's awesome! Why wouldn't he jump at the chance?"

Shawn looked over to where the other three men were laughing next to the grill. "Since he's a non-shifter, Max has never felt truly part of the Pack. Even though everyone respects him, Max doesn't see himself able to lead the others. I want to show him he's wrong."

"What can I do?" She hoped to be able to show Max see that he could be a great leader. "I want to help."

"You already are. He seems comfortable here. Once we find out what is going on, I think Max will see on his own that he has even more to offer."

She didn't have time to respond. A loud commotion announced the arrival of her nephews, younger brother and her sister-in-law.

Her two nephews, Kyle and Korrie, raced up the wooden steps to where she and Shawn were standing.

"Alpha! Alpha!" Kyle, the youngest at four, cried out.

Shawn crouched down to catch the small boy. "Hey there, little man!"

"Me, too!" Korrie called, jumping up and down.

Shawn easily picked him up in his other arm. It was a sight to see the two children in the embrace of their powerful leader.

Cassie leaned over and kissed both boys on their cheeks. "Well, hello to you, too."

Kyle laughed. "Hi, Aunt Cassie."

"Hi, honey," she said, hugging her sister-in-law. Peyton had been her best friend since grade school. When Peyton and Jacob had gotten married, Cassie had been so happy. Peyton had always been like a sister to her and now she truly was.

Cassie accepted a quick hug from her brother. He pulled away to join the other men.

"Come on, you monkeys," Peyton said to her children. "Let Alpha Shawn breathe."

Their Alpha set the kids down, patting them one last time, then hugged Peyton and strolled toward the grill.

"Well, check out Max Lawson," Peyton murmured. "He sure is looking good."

Cassie grinned. "Uh-huh."

"Jacob tells me he's staying at your place?"

"Yes."

Peyton faced her. "And?"

Cassie laughed. She ran her gaze over the boys then back to Peyton.

"Oh, an adult conversation? Nice!" Peyton commented. "How would you boys like to play with the Legos?"

Kyle and Korrie hooted then raced over to where Alex had a small play area in the corner of the porch. The entire family enjoyed hanging out together, so Alex had made sure the boys had plenty with which to entertain themselves.

Peyton put her arm through Cassie's and pulled them even farther away from the crowd. "So?"

Cassie shook her head. "I don't really know what to say. You've seen him. He's sexy as all get out, and he seems to be a great guy as well. We kissed last night and ever since then I can't seem to get him out of my mind. Or get enough of his lips. There is just something there, you know?"

"I do, but are you ready for that? You've been fighting finding a mate for a long time."

"That's getting a little ahead of us. I don't know that I want a mate right now anyway. I've never felt any sort of connection to the men Alex likes as a mate for me. Max is different, though. I don't know what will happen between the two of us, but I do know that I have to find out. I want him, but I'm worried about scaring him off too. He might not be ready."

"Huh." Peyton frowned. "All I can say is that if you are truly interested in him, then don't give up. Let him set the pace. You'll still need to let him know you're interested."

"I guess." Cassie turned so she could watch Max.

He was standing between his brother and Alpha Shawn, talking and gesturing. His tight T-shirt stretched against his chest muscles and damn if that sight didn't make her mouth water.

Max glanced over at her and the heat in his eyes called to her. She licked her lips, watching as he followed the motion with his gaze.

Peyton bumped her arm. "Well, let's go join them."

As they made their way over, Alex declared the burgers were ready. The next several minutes consisted of everyone filling plates and grabbing new beers. The group settled at the wooden picnic table.

Cassie was filled with love. This was what family was all about. These people had come together to figure out how to protect one another and the entire Pack. She was so lucky.

She sat between Max and Alex and felt one hundred percent safe. Of course, having a successful show would really prove that she had gotten her life back after the break-in. Let whoever was responsible know that they hadn't won.

She'd felt compelled to bring Max's wolf to life for him. There was no way that she'd let that piece of art go into the show, though. The canvas of Max's wolf would be for Max alone.

Even if he wasn't able to shift into his animal, sometimes she could sense how close his wolf was to the surface. Even at a young age, she'd known that Max was different. It wasn't until the night before that she'd really started to understand, though. She'd always taken the ability to shift for granted.

Now she was seeing things differently.

There was so much more to Max than what she had first considered.

"So, I spoke with the Council and they're sending out two guards to aid us in the investigation. The leader of the Church for Humanity was arrested in Nevada, but the Council has been keeping an eye on the other locations. They've pulled out all the shifters they had undercover in the Church, though," Alpha Shawn told them. "Now they have to watch from the outside."

"What about the Coalition?" Max asked.

Shawn shook his head. "They said we can wait. The Council has dealt with the Church before and the two guys they're sending have already brought one location down. Since we want to remain in secret, we won't bring in the Coalition until we have no other choice."

This was great. At least it wouldn't lead her Pack to having to reveal themselves. There were a few humans who lived around the canyon or in town, but not many. Luckily their community was mostly made up of Pack.

"With the security measures we've taken here and in town, I'm confident about what we'll be coming up against," Alpha Shawn assured everyone.

Max's hand landed on her back and she leaned into his touch. She hoped they caught whoever was causing the trouble quickly.

The others spoke more about who could be involved and why, but Cassie just listened. She finished her burger. She accepted her bottle after Alex stood and grabbed another round of beers.

They were connecting the Church with the break-in to her studio, but Cassie couldn't really see the link. Okay, so the Church didn't like art that featured animals since they were fighting against shifters, but there was no actual proof that her art had any association with shifters at all. The Church was risking a lot to go after her. Cassie kept her head down and didn't get involved in Politics. The entire thing didn't sit right with her.

No, the culprit had to be closer to home.

She didn't realize that she'd spoken out loud until everyone turned to her. She flushed while ducking her head. "Sorry."

"No," Max said. "We want to hear your ideas too."

She glanced over at their Alpha and he nodded.

"I just don't see how the Church could know enough about me to break in."

"They would have had to be watching."

"How?" She motioned, indicating the property. "Our land isn't easy to get to. And if strangers were wandering around, someone would have scented them."

Alex and Max shared a look and she stiffened. "You don't think it's a stranger, either."

No one said anything. She glared at her older brother.

Alex sighed. "No, we don't. We do think that whoever is involved with the break-in has a connection to the Church."

"Who?"

"Your assistant," Max informed her.

"James? There's no way! I already told you that!"

"Think about it, Cass," Alex responded. "He has access to the house and studio. He knows if you're out. No one would think it was strange for him to be around, and since his scent is already familiar to us, we wouldn't notice it."

She shook her head as she stood. It wasn't possible that the sweet kid she had spent so much time with would do something as horrible as destroy her work. No way.

"You're wrong. I'll prove that you're wrong," she told them and stalked away.

Someone was following her, but she didn't look back to see who it was. Her heart ached. Cassie wasn't exactly sure why. It didn't seem right that her family, who knew James, would accuse him. James merely wanted to fit in. That was why he worked so hard as her assistant. A betrayal like that would destroy her. She'd given James everything she could as a friend. She felt guilty for not sharing her biggest secret with him.

Had these last months been nothing but a lie?

Could Cassie have let in the person who wished to take out her and an entire Pack of shifters?

She fought against letting tears fall as she was swamped with a sick feeling.

It was too much. Too much information coming at her.

All she wanted was to paint and spend time with her family. Cassie had never hurt anyone in her life. She didn't deserve this, yet here she was running away from her family because they were fighting to protect her. Cassie wanted nothing more than to shift into her wolf and let the animal take over. Too bad that even if she transformed, she couldn't get away from her own thoughts.

"Cassie! Wait up!"

She turned, allowing Max to catch up with her. He jogged forward, but she glanced away before she could get caught up in watching his impressive pecs and fine body.

"I'm sorry if we upset you." Max stopped by her side. "I don't want to blindside you if in fact James is the one responsible."

Cassie shook her head. "I won't believe it until I see proof."

"That's reasonable," he agreed.

She did look at him at those words. "Yeah?"

"Sure." He shrugged. "He's your friend and you know him better than any of us. I hope I'm wrong, but if I'm not, I won't allow him to hurt you again."

Cassie nodded. That was probably the best she could ask for. She brushed her bangs from her face. "I won't get in the way of your investigation. Just tell me when you clear him, please."

Max placed his hand over his heart. "I promise."

"Thanks." She turned back to her house. "I'm going to my studio for a while."

"I'll come get you when the Council members arrive. I want you to meet with them since they'll be staying in the main house."

She waved her hand to show she'd heard Max as she walked away. It would feel good to get lost in her art like she used to. Before this entire mess started.

Max didn't try to stop her and a part of her was disappointed.

There was another way that she could get out of her head. Getting naked and sweaty with Max would take care of her worries, but he didn't offer and Cassie didn't push.

Maybe it was better this way.

It was torture to have Cassie behind the door of her studio where he couldn't watch over her. Max knew she had a lot of destroyed work to make up for but he felt helpless.

He'd spent the early evening going through every inch of security for Cassie's house and the entire Wilson property. He'd almost gone down to the stables but hadn't wanted to leave her on her own. The house should have been safe enough, but Max wasn't taking any chances.

So, he sat on a stool at the kitchen bar, watching over the territory through the lens of his cameras.

Max had seen Jacob take his family home, Alex stalk around the grounds, and not much else. Only necessary people were around so that left Max without a lot to do but think. At least his thoughts were on the Wilson family and not going to dark places.

The chime of a text message had him reaching for his phone. A twinge in his back told him he'd been sitting for too long in the same position. It was hell getting older and Max had abused his body for too long.

They're here. They want to talk right away. Bring Cassie?

Max read the message from Alex then stood. Cassie had been working for several hours, so hopefully she was ready for a break.

Instead of strolling into her studio, he knocked loudly. She had the music on, but not loud enough to keep her from hearing.

"Yes?" she yelled.

"Are you ready to go up to the main house?" he asked. "Alex just texted."

There was a moment of silence before she answered. "Okay, just let me clean up."

He leaned against the wall, unable to force himself to give her more space. It was killing him not to be able to see her.

After waiting ten minutes, Max was about to knock on the door, but Cassie opened it and slipped through. Max pushed down his disappointment at not being able to see what she'd been working on, but Cassie's appearance distracted him.

Sometime in the last few hours, she must have run her fingers through her hair, as there were a couple of flecks of paint. There was also a cute streak across her nose. He reached forward and ran his finger over the spot. Cassie blushed.

"I can get a little messy," she told him.

"It's cute," he responded. "Looks like your muse returned."

"Yeah," she agreed. "Something must be helping." Cassie leaned forward and kissed him lightly.

Max got the impression he was that something that'd woken her muse and was extremely pleased. He wrapped his arms around her back and pulled her close when she would have stepped back. That little peck on the lips wasn't enough.

He whirled them around so her back was to the sheetrock with his body between her legs. Max leaned in hard as he expertly kissed her.

She went weak in the knees, so he used more of his weight to hold her up while plundering her mouth.

The small sounds she released were erotic as fuck and he thrust his jean-covered cock against her. God, all he wanted was to have no clothes between them. He could make her forget everything that had happened in the last twenty-four hours. Take all thoughts from her head and mark every inch of her flesh.

His phone chimed in his pocket, reminding him that they had somewhere to be.

With great reluctance, he pulled back to rest his forehead against hers. "We have to get up to the main house before Alex comes looking for us."

She groaned. "I don't want to."

"I know." Another kiss, this time quick and dry. "But we have to." It was hard to release her but Max did as needed.

"Let's get this over with so we can cuddle before bed," she suggested.

"Good idea." Max entwined their fingers before leading her toward the front of the house.

Cassie waited patiently just inside the front door as Max made certain the place was locked up tight. He grabbed his laptop from the kitchen before joining her.

Once they were on the way to the main house, Max had time to watch her. Cassie appeared much more relaxed than she'd been after dinner. It looked like the time in her studio had helped calm her.

Alex was standing on the back deck with his hands in his pocket as they came around. "There you are," he said. "I wasn't sure if I needed to send a search party."

"I was painting," Cassie replied softly.

"You were?" Alex perked up. "How's it going?"

"Good, I think," Cassie told him. "I don't think I need to replace everything that was destroyed, but I wouldn't mind adding a few more pieces. It was a good thing that I'd already had the first batch sent to the gallery."

"I agree," Alex said. "We've added twenty-four-hour security guards to make sure nothing happens there."

"Oh." Cassie seemed surprised.

"What's wrong?" Max asked her.

"I guess I hadn't thought about the possibility of something happening to the other paintings. I'm not the only one showing."

"Everything will be just fine," Alex assured her.

Cassie nodded, but the worry had returned to her eyes.

"If possible, I'd like to take a look at the gallery tomorrow," Max said. "With the show coming up, I'd like to see the space for myself and where any trouble might come from."

"I'd be happy to take you," Alex offered.

"Would that be all right with you?" Max asked Cassie.

"Sure." She shrugged. "I can't expect you to sit around the house while I work all the time."

He turned toward her. "I don't mind."

"Okay," she responded. "But it's a good idea. Plus James is stopping by in the morning, so I'll have company."

"I'll see if Peyton is free as well," Alex said.

Cassie rolled her eyes but nodded. "Fine. Now are we going to meet the Council's shifters or not?"

"Come on." Alex waved them forward. "They were just freshening up and are going to meet us in the study."

As soon as the sliding glass door was opened, Max could scent the two strangers. His senses were strong even if he couldn't shift and had saved him more than a few times.

There were indeed two men standing in the middle of the room, holding a beer apiece. From their appearance, build and stance Max knew instantly that they had a military background.

He eyed them as Alex rushed ahead to grab him and Cassie drinks.

"Hello," Cassie greeted.

The dark-haired man stepped forward with a smile. "You must be Cassandra. I'm Kurt Moore and this is my associate Clint Price."

Max bit back a growl as Cassie shook Kurt's hand. Neither his human nor his wolf side liked a strange man touching what they considered theirs.

Kurt smiled at him over Cassie's shoulder. Max had to wonder if the Council shifter didn't know exactly what he was feeling.

"Nice to meet you," Clint stated when he reached out to Cassie.

Instead of a look of understanding like Kurt had sent him, there was a twinkle of amusement in Clint's gaze.

"Thanks for coming. Call me Cassie, and this is Max Lawson," Cassie introduced.

"Alex gave us a run through of everything you've organized. For not being trained as a security expert, you've done an amazing job," Kurt said.

"I appreciate it," Max responded as he shook Kurt's hand. "I just want to make sure Cassie stays safe."

"Hopefully we can help with that." Kurt motioned toward the furniture.

Max sat on the couch and pulled Cassie down to his side. Kurt and Clint booth chose chairs as Alex finished grabbing the drinks.

"We've found that the Church for Humanity had a chapter in Lubbock," Kurt started. "That's about, what…two hours from here?"

"Just about," Max responded.

"Our reports state that the chapter is closed down. We think they're just getting smarter. By taking down Dan Carter and several of the higher-ups in the Church, we lost a great deal of contact with the smaller factions. That doesn't mean they're any less dangerous."

"Is that what you'll be doing?" Max questioned.

"Yes," Kurt replied. "I don't think the Church is gone. I believe they just went into hiding. They want to stay off the grid until they make their mark. That might be what's going on here."

"What do you mean, 'make their mark'?" Cassie asked.

Kurt glanced at Clint before turning to face Cassie and Max. "It's a possibility that they will attack the gallery on the night of the show. That they plan to make a statement by targeting a well-known establishment."

She gasped. Max gripped her hand, hoping to soothe her.

"I hate to say it, but it was smart to call us," Kurt said. "The break-in to your studio has me both concerned and confused."

"Why's that?" Max asked.

"If they'd left you alone, we wouldn't have any suspicion regarding the show," Clint stated. "By attacking here, the entire Pack is on guard."

"It's like someone wanted to warn you," Kurt finished.

Max glanced over at Alex and saw him shaking his head. That made a little more sense to Max, as well. James was a close friend to Cassie and, if she was in real danger, he might risk warning her. Max strongly believed that James was responsible for the damage to Cassie's studio.

"I know what you're thinking," Cassie said. "But it's not James."

"If James is involved in the Church, he might not feel safe telling you about the threat. But the loss of your work—"

"No!" Cassie rose, cutting Alex off. "I've seen how hard James has worked. He has his own art that will be featuring."

"Then maybe that's the reason he wants to stop the attack on the gallery," Max said gently.

"I can't believe this," Cassie mumbled. She dropped back down on the couch. "I don't want to think that my friend would be so...cold."

God, this was breaking her heart and Max couldn't do anything about it.

"Tell us about James," Kurt requested.

Cassie folded her hands in her lap. Alex sighed.

"Please," Kurt pushed.

"I hired James six months ago to work as Cassie's assistant," Alex explained.

As Alex brought the two Council shifters up to speed, Max leaned against Cassie's shoulder.

"If I can prove that James is innocent, I'll do it. You'll be the first to know."

She nodded. "But what if he's not?"

That was the right question.

"Then you'll move forward. You'll know that you tried to help the young man and nothing that happens is your fault," Max said.

"I don't think it'll be that easy," she responded.

"I know. But I'll be by your side the entire time. You're not alone."

"I'm not alone," she repeated. Cassie tucked herself up under his arm and Max tightened his hold. He couldn't protect her from what had already happened. He couldn't guard her heart against James's betrayal, if it came down to it. But he could help her pick up the pieces.

In the meantime, maybe she'd be the one to help him heal his own wounds.

It'd only been a few days since he'd first caught sight of her, but Max felt more like his old self then he'd felt in years.

Chapter Five

It had been three days since the barbecue and Max was finding Cassie both intriguing and irritating.

She refused to talk to him about James or the break-in. Alex had warned him that she would act this way, but Max just didn't get it. Cassie had no problem discussing what they were investigating and had met the two wolf shifters the Council had sent. However, she wouldn't hear of James being involved. She just told him that she was willing to listen when he had solid proof.

Proof. Max was having a hard time tying James to the Church but couldn't eliminate him as a suspect, either. Max found himself more frustrated by the day. He hadn't had the opportunity to check out the gallery, either.

With Kurt and Clint in town and searching for any trace of the Church members, it'd been suggested that his visit wait a few days. He was finally getting a chance to visit the gallery the next morning. He felt better about all the waiting he'd been doing, although his anxiety had picked up quite a bit with the lack of answers over the last few days.

Max didn't allow Cassie to see any of it, though. She spent most of her time in her studio and Max was glad to see she was back doing what she loved. They'd also made a habit of sitting together on the porch late each night, talking and sharing a few kisses. They were growing closer each day.

Max hoped that was helping Cassie put the events in the past behind her as much as he was benefiting from the time together.

During the day, with Cassie working, he hung out with his Alpha, Alex and Chase. He was beginning to feel like the man he used to be. Even though he knew the camaraderie with the other three men was helping him, it was really Cassie to whom he attributed the change. He wanted to be the man she deserved.

He hated to leave her every time he ushered her inside and into her bedroom. He just wasn't sure they were ready to move their relationship to the next step. Oh, it wouldn't be long. He ached to have her against him. But she was busy, and he wanted to ensure her safety above everything else.

Getting to know Cassie better by keeping their relationship at a slow pace had the added benefit of making Max feel like he really knew Cassie. Max found that Cassie was a talented, smart and warm woman. While she didn't like to be in a group of people in strange surroundings, she loved to be with family and enjoyed gatherings with them.

She spoke to her brothers and sister-in-law at least once a day. He liked that they were so important to her.

The more Max learned about her, the more he liked her. He'd started to connect to her right away and over the last couple of days, he'd started to fall for her. Their connection was more than just sex, especially since they hadn't had it yet.

The nightmares that he'd been plagued with since he'd returned home had eased. The last two nights, Max had dreamed of some good times with his team. That in itself was a miracle which he attributed to Cassie.

Cassie asked lots of questions about what he'd done in the Navy and his friends. Out of all the stories he'd shared, he hadn't been able to talk about losing Evan just yet. But he spoke of his best friend, glad that she seemed to want to listen. And he'd needed to tell someone else about the man who'd grown to be a brother to him.

It was nice just relaxing on the patio with her.

His wolf did not fully agree. Every time Max was close enough to smell Cassie, his animal wanted to claim her. The human part of him understood that Cassie needed time to get to know him better, but the wolf wanted to mate.

As he locked up the house and checked the security, Cassie's shower turned on farther back in the house. His cock, which had been half-hard the entire time he'd sat talking with her, grew even more so. He palmed himself, thinking about how she would look, naked and wet, under the hot spray.

He bit back a moan and yanked his hand away. He'd jacked off every single night since he'd started staying with her. Tonight would be no different. He needed to get to bed. It was already after midnight. Hopefully Cassie would be turning in soon, too.

She'd gotten only a few hours' sleep before she'd risen to start painting again. It seemed to Max that she got very little rest, but she assured him it was normal for her. She painted when she could and, once she was done, she would be able to catch up on her sleep.

Max worried she wasn't taking proper care of herself, but he also didn't want to interfere. At least not yet. Once she belonged to him—not if but when—he'd demand she take proper care of herself.

He closed his bedroom door behind him and pulled his T-shirt off. Walking around the end of the bed, he folded the comforter back before dropping his shorts and boxers. He didn't always sleep in the nude even though he was more comfortable that way. However, he'd found that with Cassie close by, the need to jack off every night was strong and the only way to really calm himself enough to fall asleep.

He climbed into the big bed and lay on his back. The overhead fan turned silently, creating a soft breeze. Max ran his hands down his chest and played with his nipples. The pull made his cock even harder. Keeping the fingers of his left hand busy, he used his right to stroke himself.

It felt good, like it had the past several nights, but Max still wanted to experience what Cassie's talented fingers would do to him.

He sped up his movements as he thought about Cassie climbing into bed with him. What she would feel like under him. He thrust his hips up, imagining being buried deep inside her. He craved to hear the sounds she would make while he took her. He hoped she was vocal. He enjoyed a woman who didn't hide her pleasure.

Max pumped himself faster, already close to the edge.

Cassie had a small, compact body. She liked to wear soft cotton pants and tank tops while she painted. Even her cute painted toenails were a turn on for him.

And her mouth! God, she had a talented tongue. They'd kissed probably a dozen times a day and he couldn't get enough of her unique flavor.

He came, biting his lip to keep from crying out as he covered his hand with his seed. He fell back onto the sheets and panted. If just thinking about being with Cassie pushed him over so quickly, he had no idea how he would handle it when he finally got to have her in his bed.

He reached over and grabbed a handful of Kleenex to clean up the mess he'd made. He tossed them into the waste basket beside the bed then rolled over, burying his face in his pillow.

Sleep started to pull at him and he didn't fight it as he looked forward to what the next day with Cassie would bring.

* * * *

Cassie dried off with a clean, fluffy towel then pulled on a pair of sleep pants and a black tank top. She ran a brush through her hair, thinking about the canvases that she needed to have picked up.

She'd told James that she would call him once she was ready for everything to be moved to the gallery. Or when she was almost out of space. She'd avoided having her assistant out to her house since she knew that Max and Alex believed he was involved. She'd canceled the meeting scheduled several days ago, pretending to be too busy trying to catch up to see him.

James said he understood, but she was going to have to give in as she was running out of supplies.

In the meantime, she couldn't figure out if James was actually involved or not, so she decided to just avoid the entire thing. Max let her, to a point. He still told her everything that the two Council shifters were finding out about the Church close by. According to Alex, they were watching some houses in town to see if any members were showing up around the Pack. There hadn't been many signs of the known Church members and even less of the suspected.

Cassie felt both better and worse about that.

If the Church had not been involved in the break-in, then the only suspect was James. But she also didn't want to think about strangers having been in her house.

She felt safe having Max with her while she completed the last of the new projects. Each time she was on a roll, he left her alone, just making sure that she had food or a drink close by. And if she needed a break, he would sit with her and talk for hours.

The stories that he told were amazing for her inspiration. She'd made sure that Max hadn't seen any of the paintings just yet. After the show, she wanted to present them to him. She'd managed to make a series of works detailing each member of Max's unit. She knew that they weren't shifters, but she took what Max shared with her and brought them to life. She'd just completed the last one.

Evan. Who Max had said was his best friend. Each time he spoke about Evan, she could pick up on the tension and sadness inside Max. She hadn't asked, yet she was pretty sure that Evan had been killed.

If that was what had happened, it was no wonder Max had been so depressed when he'd arrived back in town.

She wanted the painting of Evan to be perfect. To reflect every feeling that Max had shared with her. The moment Max saw it, Cassie hoped that he would have a lasting, loving reflection of his friend.

Now, since she was done, she wouldn't be able to put off calling James any longer. Since Max was going to the gallery the next day, it would be the perfect time to ask her assistant over. Maybe she'd get a feeling if James was involved, if they had some time alone to talk.

She set her hairbrush down then strolled out of the bathroom connecting with her bedroom. Her soft mattress called to her, but she continued past it.

She'd been so close to finishing the entire series that she couldn't relax until she was finally done. She really wanted to spend more time with Max, but she just couldn't *not* work on her art. That was the way it was with her. When her muse struck, she painted obsessively then just stopped.

If she were going to have a relationship with Max — and she was going to make sure she got the chance — it was better the man learned her quirks now. So far, he had been very understanding.

She took the cover off her last canvas and let her gaze wander over the scene she'd created. The color and shading were just what she'd wanted.

There was just one more addition. She knew what it needed. She picked up her brush and chewed on the wooden tip. In her mind, she didn't see Evan as a wolf. No, the way Max described him, there would be a difference in his best friend.

Cassie had gone with a panther. A powerful, sleek black panther.

She retrieved the paint palette and started mixing the colors. The panther crouched low in a field of brush, its hind legs poised to jump, ready and willing to defend his friends.

Working furiously, she lost herself in her special world. She didn't have to think, just let the image in her mind out.

As her fingers started to cramp, she returned to awareness. The fog of concentration lifted and she stepped back, drawing in a deep breath.

It was perfect.

Elation swamped her.

The intelligence that was shining from the panther's crystal-green eyes looked back at her. As Max had spoken about his best friend, it was this image that she'd seen. Now she could finally share her gift with Max. Let him see how she saw the world and the people in it.

Tears of pride and exhaustion prickled and she rubbed at her eyes with the heels of her hands.

She'd accomplished what she had set out to do. Turning in a circle, she took in each piece of work. The way that Max had described each man and the stories he'd shared had allowed her to see them in an animal form and turn them into their animal counterpart.

She smiled. She couldn't wait to show Max.

But a glance at the clock on the wall showed that she had been busy. It was just after three in the morning, so she would have to wait to share her gift with him.

Now, hopefully, she would be able to sleep.

She walked to the attached bathroom and scrubbed the dry paint from her hands and under her nails.

Clean, she shut off the faucet and stared into the mirror. Now that she was finished with the series, she could take the time to decide how to proceed with Max.

There was no doubt that they wanted each another. And it was time to let him know that while she enjoyed getting to know him, she had to have him. She flicked off the bathroom light and headed toward her bed. Just as she reached it, she heard a faint noise from down the hall.

Cassie tiptoed to the door and pressed her ear against it. A soft moan, like from a wounded person, drifted to her. Quietly as possible, she pulled the bedroom door open and peeked into the corridor. The lights remained off and she couldn't sense anyone near. She paused and strained to pick up the sound again.

There! Coming from Max's bedroom.

She inched forward until she heard him cry out. Bolting to his bedroom, she grabbed the handle when she reached his door, relieved it was unlocked. After twisting it open, she rushed inside.

Max lay on his side, thrashing his head against the pillow. His long legs were tangled in the sheets as he kicked. He moaned again. Cassie couldn't stand to see him struggling in a nightmare.

"Max," she called as she crept closer.

"No!" he cried out, still asleep.

"Max, wake up! Max!" she tried again. Her knees hit the edge of the bed and she lightly shook his shoulder. "Max."

His hand grasped her wrist and he yanked her forward. Cassie fell on top of him but ended up trapped under his heavier bulk as he rolled. His hazel eyes popped open but were cloudy. She wasn't sure he even saw her.

With her free hand, she cupped his cheek. "It's okay, Max. It's Cassie. Wake up for me."

Although he had her pinned under his body and his hand was still wrapped around her wrist, he wasn't hurting her. In fact, under any other circumstances, she would have loved being in this position with him.

"Max, it's me," she repeated over and over.

He grunted, easing back. His gaze started to clear, and he blinked down at her. "Cassie?"

She smiled. "Hi."

He frowned. "What?" he asked. "Oh, God! Are you okay? I didn't hurt you, did I?"

He released his hold and sat back on his haunches.

"No," she assured him. "You didn't hurt me."

Since his breathing was still a little too fast, she rubbed his chest. "You were having a nightmare."

"Shit!" He closed his eyes. "I'm sorry."

She lifted one hand to rub his jaw. "Hey. Look at me." She smiled as he complied. "It's okay. I finally ended up in bed with you."

Cassie's words startled a laugh from Max and he shook his head. He was so embarrassed that she had heard him having a nightmare, but thankful he hadn't hurt her.

Max slowly lowered his head to let Cassie know he planned on kissing her. If she didn't want him to, she could still pull away. Cassie didn't. Instead, she lifted her head and their lips brushed.

She gasped, giving him entrance, and he took no time thrusting his tongue inside. Her nails dug into his bare shoulders as she held him tightly and moved her mouth against his. He'd gone to bed naked and knew that if he didn't put a stop to their making out, it wouldn't be long before he was begging to take her.

He tried to pull away, really, he did, but when she chased his lips with hers, he groaned and slanted his mouth over hers again.

She smoothed his hands down her body and under her tank. She arched into him while wrapping her legs around his waist. His cock was already hard and leaking.

It took everything he had to finally yank his head back. "If we don't stop…"

"Don't want to stop," she told him, gripping his nape and trying to pull him down.

Her confession had him fighting for control once again. "We don't have to do this right now."

Cassie sat up and Max was enraptured by her soft expression. "You're right, we don't. But I want you and I know you feel the same way. We're adults."

Max shook his head. "I want you for more than just sex." He needed her to understand that she meant more to him. He wanted a real relationship.

She grinned. "I know."

He lifted an eyebrow. "And?"

"You're not going anywhere, Max. We are going to see this to the end. And I've finally got you just where I want you." She pushed him back forcing him to lie back. She threw her leg over his waist and planted both hands on his chest. "And I am going to take care of you tonight."

"Yeah?" he replied, trying to tease, but it came out breathless.

"You bet." Cassie shimmied down his body until she was between his legs. She lifted his cock and he had to bite his lips as she pumped him. He was already so close.

"I want to taste you," she said.

"Yes," he hissed out when she did just that.

She ran her tongue over the mushroom head while stroking the length. He gripped the sheet under him to keep from grabbing her head.

She looked up at him then swallowed him deep. She was so damn sexy going down on him.

"Christ!" he growled.

Humming, she pulled back up. "I love your flavor."

He wasn't going to able to survive her seduction. It took every ounce of his control to not pump his hips as she went back to sucking him. He let out a long moan as she cupped and rolled his balls with her left hand.

Cassie was expertly bringing him to the edge, so he stopped fighting it. He let go of all his tension and just closed his eyes, enjoying the pleasure she was giving him. He lifted his hips and Cassie adjusted easily to let him slide deep before backing off again.

She licked, sucked and hummed and it wasn't long until he felt the familiar tingle at the base of his spine.

"Cassie!" he called out a warning.

She only dropped down and sucked harder. Taking that as permission, he bucked and came.

She swallowed down his seed, then popped off his cock with a smile. "I knew you would taste good."

"Come up here," he demanded.

She stroked him one last time, causing him to hiss again, then complied.

As soon as her body covered his, he rolled her under him before devouring her mouth. He was astonished at the power such a strong woman allowed. Panting with need, she begged with her body. He could read exactly what she required of him. They were connected like he'd only been able to dream of before in his life. Max wasted no time taking off her clothes as she shook. She moved with each touch, coming live under his hands. Once he had her bare and stretched out for him, he slowly traced over her with his tongue.

Shivering and panting, she rewarded him with moans and pleading. He plunged a finger inside her wet pussy as he lowered his mouth to her clit. She screamed and convulsed, climaxing for him.

Max lifted his head and watched as Cassie gasped for breath.

He removed his fingers and slowly rose back over her. She blinked at him, grinning widely. "Wow."

He couldn't have agreed more. He kissed her once again, wrapping his arms around her and holding her tightly.

They came down from their sexual high while embracing each another. Max found that he could have stayed just like that forever. He rotated their positions, lying back with Cassie draped over his chest. He buried his hand in her short hair as she petted him.

"I'm glad you came in here," he said quietly.

She laughed. "I was going to wait until tomorrow, but then I heard you, and I had to make sure you were okay."

He nodded. "It was a bad one."

"Can you...? Do you want to talk about it?"

He wasn't sure. He'd shared stories about his team with her, leaving out the last day. He still felt unable to tell anyone about that.

"You don't have to," she said softly. "I don't mind listening if you need to talk, though."

He took a deep breath. "On my last mission, Evan was killed."

She didn't show any surprise, just patted his chest.

"We'd gotten the hostages away and were almost to the rendezvous location when we ran into another group. We managed to hold them off long enough to hide in an old abandoned house. The bullets just kept coming through. I didn't know Evan had been hit until later."

He shuddered and choked on the words.

"It's okay," she soothed.

"I remember dropping to my knee to reload and looking around the room. My team had spread out to cover all the entrances and Evan was beside me with his body in front of the people we'd saved." He sniffed. "I was so proud that even injured he'd put his life before the lives of others. I thought he would be okay. He told me he would be. Sanchez was trying to reach someone on the radio and everyone else was just attempting to cover our asses. I went back to my window to hold off the incoming enemies as best as I could."

Tears filled his eyes. He ignored them, wanting to finish. "It was an RPG, rocket-propelled grenade, right through the wall. Evan and I used our bodies to shield them."

"Oh, honey." Cassie kissed his neck.

"He lived for another two hours, in pain and still trying to do his job." It had been awful. The worst thing Max had ever been through. He hadn't been able to help Evan. He'd held his best friend's hand until Evan took his last breath. "I lost it. Just completely went crazy. If I hadn't had the shifter's quick healing, I don't know that I would have survived the gunshot wounds.

I just stood next to my team, firing until there was no one else left."

Cassie crawled over him before she gripped his chin, making his gaze meet hers. "I'm glad. Do you hear me? I'm so glad you survived and are here now."

He nodded. "Me too. For the first time since that night, I feel like I'm finally healing."

She kissed him thoroughly until his cock perked up again. He ran his hands down her body, but she pulled away. "I'd like to show you something."

"Oh, yeah?" he murmured, teasing his fingers lightly down her spine.

She laughed. "Not that. Okay, not just that."

Cassie surprised him by rolling away and landing beside the bed. She held out her hand. Confused, he took it. She pulled him up and he went willingly, wondering what she was up to.

He did enjoy the view of her naked body.

She glanced over her shoulder and winked at him. "Save that thought for later."

Gladly, he thought. One taste of her was not enough. He wasn't sure why she'd insisted they leave the bed, but he was game to find out. He wasn't surprised when she pushed open the studio door. She did spend most of her time in there.

"Listening to your stories, I felt like I knew your team," she started to explain. "But I always picture someone, whether they are a shifter or not, I picture their animal. I hope this is okay."

Max allowed her to grip his hand and pull him toward the canvas on the easel. His breath caught as he looked at the powerful panther. "Evan."

"Yes, this is how I saw him."

It was the most amazing thing he'd ever seen. It was as though Cassie had read his mind and pulled out Max's own impression of his best friend. "Cassie, this is... I..." He turned to her and urged her forward. "Thank you!"

She beamed at him. "I have more."

Max didn't want to step away from the painting Cassie had done of Evan, but he was curious to see what else she'd been working on. He followed her to where more canvases leaned, covered, against the wall and watched as she removed the cloths.

"Oh, shit!" he said, astonished. His entire team came alive in front of him. He had no problem identifying each member of his unit. The talent she had for bringing the subject out in her art staggered him. "Oh, baby."

Cassie held the covers while watching him. "You like them, right?"

"I love them," he confirmed quietly. He stepped forward and ran his finger over the snow-white wolf that he somehow he knew was Matt Wallace. "I can't believe you did this."

"For you," she told him. "After the show, I want to give them all to you."

He faced her and saw the emotion shining from her eyes. Deeply touched, he moved forward and embraced her. "Thank you." The words didn't feel like enough to express his amazement, but he would make sure she understood. Every day of their lives, if he was able.

Cassie lifted her face and their lips brushed. Max needed more, so he pressed her tighter and nibbled on her bottom lip until she opened for him. He plunged his tongue inside her mouth, his blood pumping and his heart racing as she moaned and gripped him harder.

Inside, his wolf was frantic to mate with the woman that both man and beast recognized as their own.

He ripped his mouth away. "I want you."

"Yes," she hissed while he ran his fingers down her back.

They were already naked with his erection brushing against her stomach. It would be so easy to drag her down to the floor and lose himself inside her, but he knew Cassie deserved to be worshiped and for him to take his time.

"Come on." He tried to lead her back to his bedroom.

She tugged on his hand. "Here, now."

He was helpless to resist. He didn't want to. His wolf clawed at him to make sure Cassie knew she belonged to them. Until now, he'd never felt this intense need to claim anyone.

Max brushed his thumbs over her nipples, smiling at her sharp intake of breath. He cupped her firm breasts, loving the fact that they fit perfectly in his hands. "On the floor," he commanded.

She dropped gracefully, kneeling in front of him. She rubbed his palms down his stomach while bending forward to lick the bead of pre-cum from his cock.

He gasped and bucked but didn't take advantage of her mouth like she expected. Instead, he joined her on the floor and pushed her to lie back.

Starting at her neck, he ran his tongue down her body, stopping to pay close attention to every spot that made her whimper. He wanted to learn every place that he could use to drive her crazy. By the time he reached her glistening pussy, Cassie was begging him to fill her.

He tormented her by playing with her clit and softly rubbing his fingers over her slick folds.

"Please!"

He took in her flush body and the heavy need in her features. "Turn over."

She quickly moved to obey and get on her hands and knees.

"I'm going to take you," he told her. "Claim you so you know who you belong to."

"Yes, yes!"

He grasped his shaft and slid up against her. He massaged her opening with the head of his cock.

"Don't tease," she begged. "I need you."

Max thrust deeply, causing her to cry out in ecstasy. Her inner muscles clamped down around his cock and he moaned.

Cassie pushed back against him and Max's control snapped. He pulled out slowly before driving back inside.

It was fast and furious and so fucking good that he couldn't think straight. All he knew was that it felt so right being buried inside Cassie.

He snapped his hips over and over as he drove himself closer to completion. Cassie threw her head back and screamed just as she climaxed. Max plunged inside, his body tightening, and he joined her, crashing over the edge.

Sweat dripped down his forehead to land on the back of her neck. She sighed deeply, the sound full of contentment and pleasure.

Max rolled them to the side and cuddled her close. "Damn."

Giggling, Cassie nodded. "We need to do that again."

He couldn't have agreed more. "Yeah, but now I don't think I can walk."

He pulled out then pushed on her shoulders so she would turn onto her back. He poised over her. Cassie made a sight with her pink-tinged cheeks and tangled hair. "You are so beautiful."

She snorted. "I'm sure I look it right now."

"Always," he told her, cupping her face.

She lifted her head to kiss him softly. "Come on, shower then bed."

Bed. That sounded good to him. He rose, helping her along the way. He couldn't stop running his hands over her shoulders as they left the studio. He wasn't near finished with Cassie for the night.

Chapter Six

Cassie didn't want to get out of bed. She was wide awake and alone. Max's scent still surrounded her. For at least a few days she'd have him all over her sheets, right where he was supposed to be.

She rolled over onto her back to stare up at the ceiling.

The bright morning light filtered in through a gap in the shades so it was probably mid to late morning. Cassie didn't have to get up, but she did want to see her lover before he left to go to town for the day.

Next time she'd have to tire him out enough that she woke up in his big strong arms. She tossed the comforter off before slowly sliding off the mattress. She made a quick stop in the bathroom to take care of her morning routine before dressing.

The sound of voices in the kitchen clued her in to Max still being there and that he wasn't alone. Cassie couldn't mind though when she heard Peyton praising Max on his coffee making. In truth, he made the brew too strong, but Cassie was getting used to it.

Max's laughter bounced off the walls of the kitchen as Cassie stepped inside.

"Hey!" Peyton exclaimed as she spotted Cassie.

"Ugh," Cassie complained. "Too early."

"It's after ten," Peyton responded. She sniffed the air. "Of course, if you were up late…"

Cassie pointed her finger at her best friend. Yes, she had Max's scent all over her, but that wasn't any of Peyton's business. At least not in front of her lover. She accepted the mug of coffee that Max pressed into her hand. He bent down and kissed her deep. Cassie responded with enthusiasm.

Peyton giggled, so Cassie allowed Max to pull back even though she wanted to haul him back to the bedroom and ravish him.

"I have to get going," Max told her. "Peyton is going to hang out here while I'm gone."

Max had a plan—no surprise there. "I'm going to call James and ask him to stop by."

"I'm not sure that's a good idea," Max told her.

"Why not?" she demanded.

He turned her to face him before placing both of his hands on her shoulders. "I don't want you alone with him. Not until we clear him of having anything to do with the break-in."

"I'm not alone," Cassie pointed out. "Peyton's here."

Max narrowed his eyes. "I don't think…"

"And the place is covered with cameras. It's not like he'll try anything when you know he's coming and Peyton's here." Cassie thought her argument was well thought out. Max didn't look convinced though.

She set her mug on the island before wrapping her fingers around his wrists. "Nothing is going to happen to me. But if I invite James over, then he'll think we still trust him. He'll let his guard down."

He pressed his lips together before nodding. "Just be careful."

Cassie lifted to her toes and covered his lips with hers. "Promise."

With obvious reluctance Max stepped away and walked out of the back door. Cassie waited until the door was closed behind him before facing her best friend.

"Tell me everything," Peyton exclaimed.

"Hold on." Cassie held up a finger then picked up her mug. She strolled over to the sink and dumped the too-strong brew down the drain before rinsing out her cup.

She quickly started a new pot, this time with the correct amount of coffee beans against water.

"Oh thank God!" Peyton said. She jumped up and dumped her own coffee. Peyton leaned against the counter next to her as they waited for the coffee to finish brewing.

Once there was enough in her carafe to refill both mugs, Cassie motioned to the back deck.

Peyton nodded.

Cassie led the way to the same wood swing that she sat in every night with Max. She took a sip of her drink then sighed.

"If you don't start talking, I'm going to tell Alex," Peyton threatened.

Cassie laughed. "Dirty play."

"I know." Peyton cackled.

"Fine," Cassie agreed. "I finally got Max in my bed."

"How was he? Good, right?"

"Of course," she said. "So good, best ever."

"I knew it!"

"The things that man did with his mouth." She shuddered. Fuck, she was getting turned on just thinking about Max.

"What things?" Peyton asked.

"Hey," Cassie complained. "I don't ask you about your sex life."

"Only because it's with your brother."

"Yes! As far as I'm concerned, you've never done anything."

"We have two kids," Peyton pointed out.

"Shut up, shut up, shut up!" Cassie demanded.

Payton nearly fell off the swing she was laughing so hard.

"I hate you," Cassie told her.

"No, you don't," Peyton responded.

Cassie groaned. She didn't. But she still wasn't going to give her details about her sex life. She did need to do one thing this morning. "I have to text James."

"I can see by the look on your face that you're dreading it."

"I just don't know what to do about him," she confessed.

"Do exactly like you told Max," Peyton suggested. "Ask him over and act as naturally as you can. You don't know he's guilty and he's your friend. Give him the benefit of doubt."

"And if I'm wrong?" Cassie knew she could talk to Peyton about her concerns. If she brought up any of her suspicions to Max or Alex they would run with them. Peyton would listen and advise. Sometimes a girl just needed her best friend.

"Then I'll kick his ass myself," Peyton quipped.

Cassie doubted Peyton was teasing.

"Fine." Cassie pulled out her cell phone and sent a quick text to James, asking if he had time to stop by.

She'd barely taken one more sip of coffee before James's eager text that he'd be there soon arrived. Cassie glanced over at Peyton. "You're staying?"

"I'm not going anywhere."

"I guess I should get dressed," Cassie commented. She kind of didn't want to shower. The smell of Max was comforting and made her feel safe. But she was a grown woman and could take care of herself. Also, if she showered, then Max would have to rub his scent on her again once he returned.

* * * *

Max followed Alex through the gallery in complete awe. The business that Alex ran was just beautiful, the lighting arranged to showcase each work of art. There were paintings, sculptures, metal work and so much more. Max had never seen anything like it.

This show that Alex was putting on might be for a Texas city, but Max thought that it would give places like New York or Los Angeles a run for their money.

"Wow, man," Max finally said after Alex finished the tour.

Alex grinned. "Awesome, isn't it? This is the biggest show we've put on. All the artists are local. We have people coming from all over the States."

"This is a bigger deal than I realized." Hands on hips, Max ran through all the possible ways that someone or a group of people could keep from the big night from happening. After reading the reports provided by Kurt and Clint about previous attempts from the Church

Max's biggest concern was a fire. A fire would wipe out all the art and keep them from opening.

Even though there was round-the-clock security, it would take just one slip from the team and the entire gallery would be destroyed.

"I can see the worry on your face," Alex commented.

"Cassie will be devastated if anything else happens," Max said.

"We're doing everything we can."

"I know. I just feel helpless, I guess. There's been no activity at the ranch and we can't find the members of the Church. There's no way they've given up."

"No, they haven't," Alex said. "I think we're all in agreement they'll attack the gallery. The show is upcoming, so we just need to keep an eye out and stop them."

That was not what Max wanted. He wished to take the fight to the humans who thought they could hurt Cassie and the other artists. Cassie was sweet and cared about others. She hadn't done anything to have the humans' hatred turned toward her. "Nothing more on Cassie's assistant?"

Alex shook his head. "We've found a loose thread between James and an uncle, but we're not sure that makes James guilty. James claims not to have any family in town, so that's a lie, but we haven't found a single time James has had contact with his uncle. Maybe James doesn't even know."

"Or maybe they're smart," Max pointed out. "Keeping James away from his uncle who's a known member of the Church."

"I interviewed James," Alex said. "I put him in close contact with my sister."

"This isn't your fault either," Max assured him. "You were doing what you thought was best."

"She didn't even want an assistant. I pressured her into it."

Max held back a growl that wanted to escape. Not only was Cassie hurting, but Alex was taking the entire situation onto himself when he was innocent of having done anything wrong. Max would get to the bottom of this and help the Wilson family heal.

His own problems could be pushed back. The feelings of never fitting in or being enough didn't matter when he had people he needed to protect.

"From what Cassie's told me, she appreciates what James has done for her. She's happier being in the studio."

"That's true," Alex agreed.

"Then you did what was best for her. Even if James is responsible, you knew what she needed and provided it."

"Thanks, man," Alex said. He looked around the large gallery floor. "Do we need to have the talk?"

"The talk?" Max asked, although he had an idea of what Alex meant.

Alex grinned. "You know, the whole 'what are your intentions with my sister?' talk."

Max narrowed his eyes. "Yeah, I don't think so. I should probably tell Cassie about my intentions first."

"Good answer," Alex complimented. "But I just have one thing I need to say."

Max faced Alex. He wouldn't back down, no matter what Alex had to get off his chest. Max might not be the best option for Cassie. He had a lot of baggage, but he'd treat her right. He'd let her shine with what was obviously the love of her life. Not only was she talented, but he sensed the great need inside her to create. He could stand beside her as she wowed the world and protect her when needed.

"I've wanted Cassie to settle down for a long time. I've tried to get her out of the studio and on dates. I'm glad that none of those guys worked out. When I think of Cassie in the future, happy and loved, I can see you. I hope it's you."

Fuck! Alex had just said the words that Max craved to hear. That he might in fact be good enough for Cassie. Unable to speak past the lump in his throat, Max nodded.

Alex slapped him on the back. "Let's meet with the security. See what we can do to ensure our girl's big night."

"Sounds good," Max managed. He followed Alex into the back office where the camera monitors had been set up. There were two shifters inside, keeping an eye on things. Another three shifters were out taking turns securing around the block. Alpha Shawn was taking no chances and Max respected the man even more.

He'd almost not returned home to his family. A couple of his friends had decided to take a European backpacking trip. Max had almost accepted the invitation to join them. He'd called Chase to talk to him and instead of him telling his brother he wasn't returning right away, Chase had convinced him to come home. Max was glad that he'd made the trip back to the Canyon now. If he was in Europe, he wouldn't be here protecting Cassie and getting to know her better. It appeared that fate was finally giving him a break.

* * * *

"I'm glad you could make it." Cassie hugged James. For the first time in days, Cassie felt her resolve return when James embraced her back. It was good that she'd invited James to the ranch so she could talk to him. Not having contact with her assistant was allowing doubts to creep in.

James beamed at her before waving to Peyton. "Of course I came. I called Alex and he said that you're making real progress. I'm glad. I thought you'd take some time off."

Cassie nodded. "It's hard to think about what happened. I feel so violated."

Compassion showed on James's face and Cassie knew she was right about her assistant. He wasn't involved.

"I can't even imagine," James said. "And all that work…"

"Well, Cass is moving ahead of what happened," Peyton spoke up.

"That's great!" James took Cassie's hands in his. "So the company took care of the mess. I didn't see it, but Alex said it was pretty bad."

"Yeah, good as new," Cassie confirmed. "Come see the new stuff."

She pulled James along the hall with Peyton following behind. Her sister-in-law really wasn't going to allow Cassie to be alone with James for even a moment. All the other doors in the house were closed except for her studio. If James didn't already know that Max was staying with her, there was no reason to bring it up. She'd wait to see if he said something.

"I noticed the cameras out front. It looks like Alex beefed up security," James commented.

"He had to," Peyton said. "Not only is this Cassie's studio, it's her home, too. The cops have a few leads they're following up on, but until the person is caught, it's all hands on deck up here."

"It's good…that the police have leads though," James said. "Do they know why?"

Cassie shook her head. Alex had told her how to answer this question. "It could be professional jealousy. Someone who wanted into the show but didn't get the opportunity."

"That'd make sense," James said. "If they took out your work, they might think they'd be able to fill in the space."

"It's possible," Cassie said.

"What else could it be?" James asked.

Cassie glanced at Peyton quickly but shrugged at James's question. This was what Alex wanted her to say, but she felt weird bringing it up. She'd never discussed shifters with James. Not even when the shifters had first announced their presence. "The other thought is the nature of my work."

"What about it?"

Cassie peered at James. "I'm famous for my representations of wild animals. According to my brother, quite a few shifters have purchased my work. He's concerned that I might have been targeted for that reason."

She didn't miss the way James's eyes widened or how he paled. His scent wasn't quite fear, but there was something off. "I guess I never considered that. I know you sell a lot of pieces but I've never thought about who might buy them."

"Me, neither," she said. "As long as my work is appreciated, that's all I care about."

"But it's a concern," Peyton stated. "Which is the reason for the additional security for Cassie."

"Maybe you shouldn't be here alone," James suggested. "Even with Alex close by you could still be targeted again. I could stay here if you wanted. I'd stay out of your way."

"Thank you," Cassie told him. Her stomach rolled with unease. James hadn't reacted like a purely innocent party but didn't give her any more reason to suspect him. "I don't think that's necessary, though. With the cameras and my family, I'm sure I'll be just fine."

"Well if you change your mind, just let me know. It's no big deal," James said.

"I will, promise." Cassie waved her hand toward the canvasses sitting on easels around the room. "Well? What do you think."

"Oh my god!" James rushed over to the painting of Evan. "This is incredible. The best you've ever done."

Pride filled her. She knew how much Max loved the painting, but having someone else say it was great meant a lot. Max had an emotional connection with the subject. She really wanted to show Max that his friend would always be with him.

"Cassie." Peyton had a look of awe on her face. "These are really good. I saw the work that had been destroyed and while they were great these..." She waved her hand. "James is right. The best you've ever done."

Cassie had to turn away to wipe at the tears that threatened to fall as Peyton and James went from one canvas to another.

Her entire world had felt like it was crumbling down the night that she'd walked in and seen the destruction of her work and studio. Instead of focusing on what she'd lost, her family and Max had helped her move on. She'd created a whole world just for Max and everyone loved it as much as she had.

She truly was a lucky person. Cassie got to spend her day creating what she loved and her nights with the most intriguing and attractive man on the planet. This was what she'd waited for all her life. This feeling of contentment and happiness that rushed through her.

She was going to have to convince Max that she was ready to see where their relationship could go. Cassie wanted to talk about the future and what roles they'd fill in each other's lives. *Will there be children? Travel? Maybe both.*

All she knew was that in every scenario she pictured, Max had a starring role as her partner.

There was still so much to discuss, though.

Max had confided in her that he'd never felt one hundred percent part of the Pack. That would be a problem if he wanted to leave. Cassie relied on her family to keep her sane and working. Max appeared happy, though.

She'd woken him from a nightmare the previous night, so what had happened to him before he's come home was still haunting him.

He'd helped inspire her muse, so she needed to find a way to return the favor. Alpha Shawn had mentioned that he had plans for Max. Maybe Cassie could talk to their Alpha more and see what he thought she could do to help.

Even if it meant Cassie getting out more and attending more Pack events, she'd do it. As long as Max was shown that he was truly a valued member of the Pack, Cassie would do anything.

"What's this one?" James started walking toward the covered painting in the corner of the room.

"No!" she shouted.

James stopped then looked at her in confusion.

"Sorry, that one's not ready," Cassie lied. She didn't want anyone to see the painting she'd done of Max's wolf. That was just for the two of them to share. She hadn't even shown it to Alex or Peyton. It was too personal. If James got a look, he'd insist she put it in the show and that was not going to happen.

"Oh sure," James said. "I understand." He peered around. "I'll have the gallery come and pick up the ones ready. We'll need to decide where to place them, but I think they should be the focal point of the show. They're that amazing."

"Thank you," Cassie told him.

"But maybe you should think about what Alex said."

"What?" Confused, she glanced back at her assistant.

"Well, he mentioned that a lot of shifters are buying your work. I can see why, looking at these paintings. Maybe you should stop for a while. Try to concentrate on something else. You do beautiful landscapes as well."

"You think I should stop painting animals?" she asked, shocked. Surely James understood that she didn't have a choice. If she tried to force a change, she could end up with nothing at all.

"I think it's worth a try. It would keep you off the shifters' radar and keep you safe."

That wasn't what she wanted to hear. Maybe Alex and Max had been right about James. The entire afternoon was becoming to feel like a big disappointment. She'd gone back and forth so many times on whether she thought James was guilty. Instead of getting an answer she was happy with, Cassie was even more confused than when James had first arrived.

"How about I make some lemonade and you two can discuss arranging the pick-up for tomorrow?" Peyton suggested, no doubt picking up on her chaotic thoughts.

"Sounds good," Cassie answered. She pasted on a smile and motioned for James to precede her. She didn't feel comfortable turning her back on her assistant.

Chapter Seven

Excitement filled Max as he helped Cassie climb onto the back of his bike. It had been her idea for the two of them to take a ride lower into the Canyon and have a late-night picnic. It was a fucking fantastic plan and he was looking forward to seeing her under the full moon.

Several of the Pack would be out in their shifted forms, but Cassie had informed him that she had a place that would be completely private for the two of them.

His entire life, Max had hated the night of the full moon.

As a child he'd known the importance and had looked forward to his first shift. Then, as he'd gotten older, it'd become obvious that there was something wrong with him. No one knew why some of the shifters could transform or why Max was one of the few that didn't. His parents had tried to find answers for him, sending Max to every Pack doctor who thought they could help. In the end Max was dubbed a non-shifting shifter. A title he had to live with.

Once he was old enough to leave the Pack, he'd joined the military. That way he didn't have to watch as his family and friends enjoyed the full moon, or keep them from running just to stay with him.

In all the excitement around the Wilson property, Max hadn't been paying attention to the calendar or what night it was. Cassie, on the other hand, had figured out a way that the two of them could be together outside on this important night.

Max knew the moment she'd announced her idea that it would be too easy to fall in love with her. Putting his needs before her own, Cassie had proved she was the woman for him.

Cassie didn't normally shift with the Pack, anyway. She'd sent most of her family off. There were still half a dozen guards taking shifts to protect the Wilson ranch. They'd all get to transform at some time during the night, but no one who wasn't supposed to be there would get onto the property.

The security around town was in full force as well.

If humans were looking to catch a shifter that night, they'd be highly disappointed. Alpha Shawn had been very specific to the Pack on where they could and could not shift.

Cassie wrapped her arms around his waist, sending jolts of electricity down to his cock. He could smell the leather from the jacket he'd made her wear. It was a little big on her, but Max liked knowing that she was protected by something that was his. Plus, his scent would be all over her when she took it off.

If he had his way, Cassie would always be covered in his scent.

"Ready?" he called back.

Cassie squeezed his middle. "Yes! Take me for a ride."

Max turned the ignition, bringing his motorcycle to life. The rumble of the engine under him was familiar and settling. Cassie gave a squeak, and he grinned. Yeah, the power she felt would amp up the arousal he already smelled on her.

He released the brake before pulling away from her house.

The Wilson ranch was located deep inside the national canyon, on the private residence side, so he wouldn't have to go through any of the State entrances. He had spent hours of his childhood climbing, hiking and getting to know the canyons. Even with a Pack of wolf shifters close by, there were still natural predators in the area, so they did have to be careful. The last thing Max wanted was for their night to be interrupted by a hungry or curious cougar.

No, Max would give Cassie this perfect night.

There were promises that he couldn't make. Max wished he'd been able to promise her that James wasn't involved in the break-in. Or that she'd never be targeted again. It'd been on the tip of his tongue to say that everything would be all right as long as he was by her side. Instead he had to stand and watch her rebuild a promising show she'd been so excited about.

As he drove down the long, winding road, she rested her cheek on his back. Max slowed to see more of the view. The sun would be setting by the time they arrived at their destination. He planned to be holding Cassie when that happened, but she'd timed their trip well. He could postpone a few minutes so the scenery didn't fly by too fast.

Hopefully, there'd be many more trips on his bike where he could show her how it felt to have the wind in her hair and the excitement of speed.

Cassie pointed to a gaggle of turkey on the side of the road and he grinned. If they tried to get closer, the birds would flee, but it was nice seeing how thick and fat they were. It looked like it'd been a good year for the animals in the canyon.

So much of the area relied on a sparse rainfall. This far up into the panhandle of Texas, the heat of the summer often proved to be dangerous. Luckily, the spring had brought record rain that had helped the canyon plants and wildlife.

Since he'd spent so much time in the desert during his service, the heat didn't bother Max. Even his wolf appeared to prefer hot to cold. Max hated to be chilled. He was an outdoor kind of guy. The peaceful ride reminded him that he should have gone hiking or climbing as soon as he'd gotten back. Even though he couldn't shift like the others, he felt a connection to the territory that he'd been raised in.

The land called to a part of him that was buried deep inside Max.

As Max slowed further to take the almost hidden path Cassie had told him to look out for, she squeezed his waist.

God, he was so happy right then.

The nightmares that plagued him and the horrors that he'd witnessed didn't matter. All he cared about currently sat on the back of his motorcycle, holding on tight to him.

The uneven path had them bumping along until they had gone as far as possible. Max pulled to a stop.

He turned off the engine, allowing the quiet night to settle around them.

"That was amazing," Cassie said.

He turned, taking in her flushed cheeks and wide smile. "It was."

"We have to do that more often."

Max nodded, since he'd just been thinking the same thing. "Show me your spot?" he requested.

"Yes!" Cassie used his shoulders to climb off. She pressed her breasts to his back then slid seductively against his body.

It was all he could do to keep his hands to himself. This was still a little bit too public for what he wanted to do to her.

Once she had her feet on the ground, he swung his leg off to stand next to her.

"It's a little bit of a walk, but it shouldn't take us too long to get there," she said.

"No problem," he responded. Max grabbed the bag she'd packed. He took her hand with his free one. "Lead the way."

Cassie lifted to the tips of her toes and kissed him before tugging on his hand. She was so damn cute when she was this excited. "I can't wait to show you. I found this spot on one of my hikes a few years ago, then figured out several ways to get there."

"Sounds good," he commented. Max didn't care if she took him to the ugliest spot in the entire canyon. Being with her would be beautiful.

Hand in hand, they stepped around skinny trees and large local plants. The farther west they hiked, the greener the land became. Max tried to get his bearings. He'd thought he'd been over every inch of the canyon, but he had no idea where Cassie was leading him.

"Almost there," she said.

They were making the walk in silence, not because they had nothing to stay, but because they were instead enjoying the amazing canyon around them. It was comfortable and soothing. Out here, the smile hadn't fallen from her face, either.

She tugged him around one of the large canyon walls with several cave openings then stopped.

Max's mouth dropped open. "Holy shit," he managed.

"Nice, right?" She sounded so pleased.

"Yes!" He dropped the bag before spinning around. "How did you find this place?" If Max hadn't walked in himself, he'd have sworn that they were not in the middle of a canyon in the heat of Texas.

Lush pads of grass as well as tan and red rocks peppered the small center, surrounded in every direction by huge canyon walls. If there'd been a water source close by, he'd have believed they'd been transported to some magical place.

"It's great," he told her. "Unbelievable."

She stepped up behind him. He picked up her sweet scent before her arms came around him. As Cassie rested her chin in the middle of his back, he covered her hands with his. "I'm so glad I could show this to you. I haven't brought anyone here, ever."

"Not even your brothers?" he asked. Max almost whispered. It felt as though talking too loudly would be disrespectful.

"I wanted a place that was solely mine," she confessed.

Max understood.

"Then you showed back up in my life and I knew that you would appreciate the beauty here. So, I wanted to share it with you. Especially once the sun sets."

He turned capturing her palms and holding it to his chest. The moment was perfect, unhurried and special. Max lowered his lips to hers and kissed Cassie with all the passion he felt.

Cassie pressed closer while he slipped his arms around her back. Even with the height difference, Max could stand here all night just kissing her. But she must have had other ideas, since she pulled back.

"There's a blanket in the bag," she told him. "I want you making love to me as the sun sets."

Fuck, his cock jerked. Romantic. He'd never thought of himself as someone who'd take long walks on a beach or love his woman under the stars, but God he wanted to be that guy.

"Give me a minute to get things set up." Max strolled back to the bag and grabbed it before peering around. He wanted the absolute perfect spot for this. He walked around until he knew just where he'd be making love to Cassie that night. Hopefully, all night.

He dropped to his knees on the soft patch of grass before digging around in the bag. Carefully he laid out all the items Cassie had packed. Food, drinks, lantern and finally the blanket. Max flicked his wrists, unfolding the soft red and black flannel out before laying it down. He arranged all the other items on the edge to not only hold down their covering but so the food and drinks would be close by. She'd packed cold bottles of beer, fried chicken, sides and even chocolate cake. Max planned to be eating dessert off her later.

Satisfied with how everything looked, he held his hand out to her.

Cassie had watched him, not moving from where he'd left her. The softness in her gaze gave him hope that she felt as strongly as he did. That when she looked toward the future, she pictured him by her side.

"Come here, love," he requested.

She shuffled closer, not taking her gaze from him.

Max pulled his shirt over his head before Cassie reached him. He tossed it to a corner of the blanket then pulled on her hands until she knelt in front of him.

He kissed her. Gently, at first, then adding more pressure until she opened for him. Max peppered kisses down her neck and lower as he undressed Cassie with slow and sensual movements. By the time he had her completely naked, she trembled.

"Lie back," he urged her.

With the dark red, orange and yellow blazing in the background, the sight of Cassie bared for him was remarkable.

"Keep watching me," he ordered.

Cassie nodded.

He took his time removing his shoes, socks and pants. In just his boxer briefs, Max crawled until he was between her legs.

"I want to see all of you," she said.

"You will," he promised. The erotic atmosphere was enough to already have his cock wet and there was more he wanted to do before he gave in to his own needs.

Max picked up her right foot and moved it farther to the side, opening her up so he was admiring her fully. Every inch of her soft, precious skin was his. He lowered his head before trailing his tongue along her inner thigh.

"Max," she gasped.

"I'm going to eat you alive," he warned.

"Yes," she hissed.

He chuckled against her flesh. With his left hand, he played with her clit, drawing out more pleasure. She was already wet for him as he lowered his mouth to her pussy. Licking and teasing Cassie, Max felt like the most powerful man in the world, being able to amp up her desire.

"Oh, please," she begged.

Max knew what she wanted. However, this was a time he'd enjoy her body without worrying about his needs. Adding a finger along with his tongue, Max went about gratifying her until Cassie was scratching and yanking at his hair. Still he didn't stop. Not until she released a rough shout and climaxed.

He lapped her juices, enjoying the sweet taste.

"I need you," she moaned.

"I know," he responded. Max sat up on his knees, still light-headed from how overwhelmed he felt. He palmed his shaft, trying to relieve some of the pressure.

Cassie sat up enough to cover his hand with hers. "Please."

Hell, yeah. "Roll over," he ordered. The final rays of the sun were in the process of disappearing and he didn't want to miss it.

She flipped onto her stomach before raising onto her hands and knees.

Max caressed her smooth, flawless left ass cheek, then her right.

"Look up," he demanded. "When the sun dips below the canyon, I'm going to be inside you."

She shuddered.

"I'm going to make love to you in the minute that day turns to night. This is going to be our ritual. We'll do this every month. Me and you."

Cassie whimpered. "I want that so much."

Jesus, how can she be so perfect? "You'll have it." Max pushed his boxer briefs down his hips before he kicked them off. He grasped the base of his cock, teasing it between Cassie's slick folds as he peered up into the sky. *Soon.* He'd be inside her soon.

"Max," Cassie whined. She wiggled, trying to speed things along.

"Bad girl," he teased. He lightly slapped her on the ass. "Behave."

The sound she let out, between a laugh and growl, was cute. He wasn't going to tell her that as she began threatening him.

"I'll lay you back and take what I want," she told him. "Ride you until the moon is full and over us."

Not that he didn't like her idea, but there'd be time for that later. The picture that he had in his head, though, was one he would make come true.

"It's time," she told him.

"Not yet." Max stroked his cock against her. "Almost." It was hard not to give in and push his way inside.

Cassie dropped her shoulders, which pushed her ass harder against him.

"Tricky," he admonished.

"Just getting comfortable since you're intent on waiting all night," she quipped.

Max leaned down and licked a trail from her neck to her spine. He grinned as she shivered. Yeah, he knew how to make her hush. He reached for her clit again.

She was so sensitive there and he loved playing with her.

"That's fighting dirty," she complained.

He stopped moving his finger. "Do you want me to stop?"

"No," she practically shouted. "Please."

Max went back to teasing her as the time finally came. He stopped rubbing against her and held his cock tip at her entrance. He pushed in right before the sun's final rays disappeared.

"Max," she murmured.

He gripped her hips with both hands as he withdrew before slamming back inside. They rocked together while the darkness began to surround him. The sounds in the night rose until Max could only hear the best of what nature had to offer.

It was easier to connect with the animal inside when the world was coming alive.

He slid in and out over and over, keeping a steady rhythm. Cassie threw herself back, trying to get him to go faster, but Max had been serious when he'd said he'd wanted to make love to her all night long.

"Please, Max," she begged. "Harder."

He tightened his grip before thrusting at the same pace. Max wasn't giving in.

"Fucker," she grumbled.

"Keep talking," Max told her. "I'll do this until you can't see straight."

She giggled but ended it with a long groan. Max had indeed sped up for her. "Good," she said. "So good."

Yes, it is. "Hold on," Max said. "Gonna show you how good we can be together."

"Always are," she panted. "Good. Together."

Finally, he was making it too hard for her to argue...or even talk. He slammed his hips forward, drawing out each pump forward and slide back. Her inner muscles clamped around his cock, trying to keep him inside. Like he ever wanted to leave.

As much as Max intended to spend the night buried deep, he couldn't help but naturally increase his tempo until he was plunging with all his might. It was a good thing they were both shifters, or they'd be bruised the next day.

"Like that," she yelled. "Please, more."

Max hammered deep until she screamed while climaxing hard.

Sweat dripped from his forehead onto her back. He managed to tear one hand from her hip to grab at her hair. He yanked her head back then lowered his mouth next to her ear.

"Look up," he demanded. "Look at the sky."

Full night had fallen around them. It was beautiful with the first of the stars blinking into view.

"Perfect," she murmured.

"Just like you," he whispered as he finally went over the edge.

* * * *

The sky had filled with stars as the moon shone brightly above them as they lay together. The quiet of the night was so peaceful she could pretend there was no one else in the world but the two of them.

Cassie lifted her head from Max's chest before she took a long pull of her beer. It was still cold and refreshing, soothing her sore throat from her cries of passion earlier. "This is heaven. I never want to leave this place." She cuddled back down to him.

Max chuckled. "We'll eventually run out of food."

"And want showers."

"Yep," Max agreed. "Guess we'll just have to make this a weekly thing."

Cassie rolled until she could see his face. "You keep talking like you're planning to stick around after this is over. You are, right?"

He lifted his head as his eyes went wide. "Yes. I'm not going anywhere."

She searched his face. They hadn't talked about what would happen when she was safe again. He'd retired from the service, but he'd been staying with Chase. He didn't even have his own place. "We haven't talked about your plans. What are you going to do?"

Max shrugged. "I haven't decided. Chase offered me a job."

"Working in the diner?" she asked.

"That's what I was doing before you needed me," he said.

"I'm glad you were here," she said. Cassie couldn't imagine how she'd feel with someone else guarding her. She certainly would not be sharing her private spot.

"Me, too," he said. "And I'm not going anywhere."

"Promise?"

Max smiled. "Promise."

Cassie kissed him. She had to. Max ran his hands down her back, but a howl cut through the night and they pulled apart. "Not close. We're still all alone."

He was looking past her shoulder, though.

"Max," she said. "It's just someone from our Pack. They won't come down this far, though."

"I want to see you shift," he said.

Cassie felt like the rug had been tugged out from under her. She jerked back. "No."

"Cassie—"

"I wouldn't do that to you," she said. "I invited you here so that we could share this night together."

He cupped her face then drew her close. "And I love it. But I want this. I've been lying here thinking about it. I can't ask you to give up shifting on a full moon."

"You didn't—"

"Shh." Max placed his finger gently against her lips. "I want to share this with you. To see you in your wolf form. To pet you."

"I don't want—"

"Please," he asked. "Show me."

Cassie wished she knew if this was really what he wanted. Max might think that it'd be fine, but what if this drove him away? She couldn't help being able to shift any more than he could help not being able to. "If you're sure."

"I am," he responded.

She climbed up to her knees as he did the same. Cassie was already naked so that pesky chore wasn't needed.

"You're going to be so beautiful," he told her. The gentle hand that he placed on her cheek helped calm her racing heart. Max was serious—he actually wanted to see her wolf.

Cassie took a deep breath. "Okay." She kissed him quickly before moving off the blanket all together. Still kneeling, she called forth her other half. Cassie didn't think of her wolf as separate from her human side. She kept her human intelligence in her shifted form, even if her animal instincts were sharper.

She closed her eyes to concentrate, since looking at Max would just be a much bigger reminder that he couldn't do this. The wolf part of her rushed to the surface. It felt as if two parts of a whole were coming together.

Magic, or whatever the transformation was called, coursed from head to toe. Cassie didn't know how shifting worked, but she liked to believe that some magic was infused with her DNA that allowed such a special gift. With Max, though, she wondered what made them different from humans. Max had told her that he'd used his heightened senses in the service, so even though he didn't change to wolf form, he still wasn't fully human. The questions had never bothered her before, but now she wished for answers she could share with him.

Her spine snapped and all thought slowed down. Fur prickled up from her skin and, in the next instant, she was opening her eyes, seeing a very different world.

The transformation was quick and without pain.

Cassie shook her full body to familiarize herself with her new form before peering over at her lover.

Max was smiling at her.

She tentatively took a step closer to him. Even with her animal eyes, he was magnificent. Strong, dominant and handsome. The urge to roll over and bare her belly was strong.

It was easier to make out the different shapes in the dark with her wolf vision. Even though she'd been able to see fine before, now everything was sharper. The edges of rocks, the soft blades of grass and Max's sincere expression.

"Beautiful," he whispered.

His one-word response gave Cassie the confidence to move next to him.

He lifted a hand, slowly moving toward her, until his palm settled at the base of her neck.

"My mom," he said. "She would let me pet her for hours. I always expected her to get tired of me running my hands through her fur, but she never did."

If she could have, she'd have told Max that he could do the same with her. Like she'd ever complain about having his hands on her. In any form.

"Can you come lie across me?" he asked.

Cassie did as requested, laying her head across his legs with her body on the blanket.

"Thank you," he murmured.

She closed her eyes as Max smoothed a hand from her neck down her back. His fingers were gentle while pressing against her skin.

The full moon hung above them and now Cassie felt perfectly at peace. She in her wolf form, with her mate attending to her. *No, not mate*, she had to mentally correct herself. She might care for Max and could see herself falling in love with him one day, but it was too soon to even consider mating.

Or is it?

Earlier, Max had claimed that he had no intention of leaving. He was happy there with Cassie. So maybe it was too soon to think about children or declaring their love, but that didn't mean she couldn't fantasize about nights in the future. Little trips to her special spot in the canyon where the two of them could be together. Nights wrapped around each other, locked in an embrace and lost in a world that belonged to just the two of them.

She sighed deeply, warming at the thoughts in her head.

Cassie didn't know how long she lay over Max's lap as she drifted. The air around her stayed comfortable with no hint of rain, so there was no chill to bother her.

All too soon, when she was about asleep, Max kissed the top of her head.

"How about you change back now? That way I can pet you with more than my hands."

She lifted her head to peer at him before giving a really big yawn.

Mac chuckled. "Did I about put you to sleep?"

Cassie nodded.

"How about I wake you back up?" Max offered. He nudged the bottom of her chin with his nose. "Come on, baby."

Okay, it'd be worth it to transform back to have him touch her in her human form. Cassie hefted up then took a few stumbling steps away. The scent of small critters and prey didn't entice her to hunt. It was Max's woodsy smell that propelled her to hunker down. She pictured her human body, her feet, ankles, knees, legs. The change was upon her and in only a few moments, she was on her hands and knees, panting.

Max dropped down next to her.

Cassie hadn't realized he'd followed her.

He pulled her into his arms, smoothing a hand over her shoulders.

"Thank you," he said. "Thank you for showing me. You are the most gorgeous creature."

"Touch me," she said. She yanked his head down so she could reach his mouth. "You promised."

"Yes, I did," he responded, picking her up. Max carried her back to the blanket and laid her down gently.

"Don't tease this time," she begged. Cassie had enjoyed every second of when they'd made love earlier, but she needed him. Wanted him, right that moment.

"I won't," Max answered. He kissed her and covered her body with his.

Cassie wrapped her legs around his waist before digging her heels into his lower back. She arched up so that his hard cock was pressed against her.

"Oh yes," she murmured while he rocked against her.

"Hang on to me," he ordered. "We're going for a ride."

Cassie laughed in delight.

Chapter Eight

Cassie wrapped the canvases up one more time so they could be taken to the gallery. The acrylic paint was already dry and ready to be picked up. She'd called James, confirming what time he'd to come by to set up a delivery time. He would be there any minute and she was hoping that he would be gone by the time Max returned.

Just thinking about Max brought a smile to her face.

After the night before, she found herself longing just to see him. Making love on the trip deeper into the canyon and later back in her bed should have worn them out. Still, any time that Max touched her, Cassie was ready for more of him. All she could get. They'd spent most of the morning in bed and it wasn't until Alex had phoned asking Max to meet him at the stables that the two had managed to get up.

Max was a passionate lover and she could honestly say that she'd never been with anyone who was so intent on ravishing her. She was pleasantly sore as she moved around the studio.

Now that she was finished with the last of her series, she could enjoy a few days just to explore what was happening between her and Max. The show was coming up fast, but there wasn't anything else for her to do except show up.

Instead of worrying about the show, the gallery or the break-in, she was making plans about showing Max everything she loved. He'd said he was sticking around, but Cassie wanted to share with him her favorite places to entice him further. They planned to ride the horses into the canyon in the late afternoon. Very, very secluded spots. She looked forward to getting Max horny and naked again.

Laughing at that thought, she squealed when someone touched her arm. She whirled around, heart beating frantically. "Shit!"

"Sorry!" James held up his hands. "You were lost in your own world."

She blushed. *Isn't that the truth?* "It's okay. I was just thinking."

"Good thoughts, apparently, since you're blushing."

She nodded. Not that she was going to tell James anything. Max might not know for sure whether James was guilty or innocent, but he'd remained suspicious of her assistant. Cassie had admitted to the weird feelings she'd had about James's visit, but now that she had time to think about it, Cassie wanted to laugh at herself. James had always been quiet and a tad off. Just a weird little artist, much like her. There was no reason to wonder about James. One of the reasons she'd asked James to oversee the pick-up from the delivery company to the gallery was to prove to Max and her brother that James could be trusted.

"I appreciate you coming." She changed the subject. "I'll just feel better knowing you're with the new work. No chance of anything else happening."

James grinned. "I can't believe you got so much done in just a few days." He took in the covered pieces around the room.

"Me neither," she confessed. "I wasn't even sure I was going to add any more to the show. I'd only lost two pieces and we have enough to go forward, but I just…got inspired."

James sighed. "It's unbelievable what you can do."

"Hey." She didn't like the sadness she heard in his tone. "You are just as talented. This is going to be a great first show for you."

"No, it's not."

Cassie frowned, walking toward him. He'd gone from sad to anger so fast. Nerves could do that, though. This was his first big show, so it was natural to believe this would be his only chance. But Cassie had confidence in him. "James, I promise it's going to be okay. Better than okay, actually, you'll see."

"Don't," he snapped and held up a hand to stop her. "You know, I thought this was going to be so easy."

Unease tingled down her spine. Okay, maybe this wasn't about the gallery show after all. He was also more than a little angry. This wasn't good. "What? What was supposed to be easy?"

"All I needed to do was find out as much as I could about you and your family. I couldn't believe it when you saw my work and thought it was good. And then Alex! He offered to show some of my pieces!"

"Of course," she replied cautiously. "Because you *are* talented. He wanted to give you a chance."

James shook his head as he reached behind his back. Cassie gasped at the sight of the black gun.

"Wha… What are you doing?" *Shit.* Max wouldn't be back for a while. He'd been right about James—everyone had—and Cassie hadn't wanted to see it.

"I didn't actually think you'd do it. Be able to replace the paintings. But they are even better than the first ones you created. This is all your fault."

Cassie knew it was stupid to argue with an armed madman, but she had to try to keep James talking. Maybe someone would come check on her. "Let's just talk about this."

"Don't try to play me," James said. "We need to go. I doubt we have much time before that man comes back."

"No, I—"

"I didn't come inside until your bodyguard left. I know we're alone right now. Just follow my instructions and I won't have to hurt you."

"James, you don't have to do any of this. We can talk to Alex. If you want more to do with the show, he can help you. I'll help you. Please!"

"But I do. You see, the show is never going to take place. Right now, a couple of my cousins are at the gallery, and in just a little while, there will be nothing left of the building. The fire should burn pretty damn hot with all the supplies we keep in the storage room."

Cassie started shaking. How could she have misjudged James so badly? He gazed at her with bright eyes that showed traces of a craziness she'd never witnessed before. Even the way his voice was pitched higher scared her.

"The fire here shouldn't be as bad. Maybe there'll be something that can be saved. I don't figure your brother or bodyguard will be far," James said.

Her house, the studio—everything that she had was in this man's hands. Inside, her wolf instincts were screaming at her to fight. She could take out this threat to her and her own. If she shifted, James would know the truth and was more likely to kill her than anything else.

He waved the gun toward the doors. "But we won't be here to find out what they can save. Start moving."

"Where are we going?" Cassie knew better to get in a car or leave with someone attempting to take her. That was on every crime drama she'd seen.

"Some people want to talk to you. They know you're familiar with some shifters. Hell, they even tried to convince me that you're one. I told them that was crazy, but I can't deny that there is something about your art that draws the monsters to you. I cataloged where all your paintings have been shipped. Several pieces have gone to known shifters."

Of course they had. Cassie knew where every piece had ended up. The fact that James did too was unsettling. "You're working with the Church for Humanity?"

James snorted. "I've been a member all my life. My uncle leads the division here in Texas. Since Bruce Carter and the California chapter have been arrested, it's up to us to stop the madness of people accepting the shifters. I mean, can you even imagine someone being able to turn into a wolf or some other kind of animal?" He visibly shuddered. "Horrible."

Cassie was shocked that James felt that way. On one hand, it was probably in her best interest that he didn't believe she was a shifter, but she wanted to set him straight that they were not monsters. The more information that came to light about shifters, the more people who'd initially been scared were now accepting of them.

"Anyway, we'll stop the show. There were going to be several shifters who have already RSVP'd, and we don't want their kind in town. After you talk to my uncle and tell him what he needs to know, he'll let you come back, if you promise to stop supporting the shifters. They shouldn't be able to buy your work. They're...they're just animals, really. Your art is too good to be wasted on them!"

Cassie knew damn well that if the Church got hold of her, she would not be coming back home.

"And you're going to burn my house and gallery down?"

James nodded. "It's the only way we can ensure Alex doesn't go on with the show. I don't know how long you'll be gone." He shrugged. "But I'll make sure they know you're okay."

"James—"

"Now, we really do have to go. My friends should be here any time to set the fire and we don't want to be anywhere near here when it goes up."

"You're talking about burning my house down!"

"Shh!" James stomped toward her. "I know and I'm sorry, but it's the only way! Now hurry up, we have to leave." He grabbed her shoulder and shoved her forward. "I wasn't kidding when I said it was time to go."

Cassie shuffled her feet as she was propelled toward the balcony door. She knew she had to figure out a way to get Alex or Max's attention, but her mind was racing and she couldn't think straight.

James pressed the muzzle of the gun against her arm and she considered turning and trying to grab the weapon. Even if the gun went off, there was a good chance it wouldn't kill her. Plus, if Max or Alex heard the shot, they would come for her.

"Don't try anything," James whispered. "My brother is over at your nephews' house and we really don't want to hurt the kids."

Oh, God! The fight that had been building burst and she sagged. Cassie didn't want to believe him, but what if they were prepared to get hold of the boys? She nodded and unlatched the double doors. She'd just have to play along. They didn't know she was a shifter. Not yet, anyway. If Cassie acted like she was cooperating, maybe that meant she'd get out of this alive.

"Head straight for my car."

Once she'd pushed open the doors, she saw that James had parked close by. There was not a lot of room to form a plan before she would be inside his vehicle. No way for her to call for help.

James nudged her with the gun again. "Walk."

Her bare feet didn't make a sound when she crossed over the small deck and down the couple of steps. She looked around, hoping someone, anyone, would be close by. Instead, all she could see was the empty yard.

She'd fought against the protection and cameras and what good were they doing her now? "James, this isn't going to work. Let me get Alex and we can talk this through."

"Talk?" James stated. "So you or your brother can try to sway me to the side of the shifters? I don't think so.

After you talk to my uncle and hear what he has to say about them, you'll understand. I told him you didn't know any better. He'll help you."

She didn't know what James' uncle thought he knew, but it was obvious that James believed the man's preaching.

The grass was cool and moist under her feet. She stopped and turned to James. "He's wrong. Shifters are not monsters. They are not evil."

"I know you believe that. If you knew what they were planning, how they're going to enslave us humans, you wouldn't defend them. There's so much you have no idea about."

"Listen to me!" she said desperately. "The Church—"

"Stop!" James snapped. "Just get to the car."

Cassie dropped her hands and turned back around. She almost wept in relief as she saw Alex step into view.

"Shit," James muttered. "Just act natural. I'll take him with us if I have to, but my uncle will not be pleased."

The gun was jammed harder into her and she hissed. Alex would be able to smell her fear—hell, he could probably hear the way her heart raced inside her chest. Still he strolled forward like he didn't have a care in the world.

"Hey, sis. Hey, James," Alex called out.

Cassie figured her brother couldn't see the weapon as he walked toward them but didn't know how to warn him.

"Hey, Alex!" James waved with his free hand. "We're just going to run into town really quick."

Come closer, Cassie mentally begged her brother.

"Cool!" Alex hollered back. "Can you stop at the gallery and pick up a box I need?"

"Uh, sure," James replied.

"Good." Alex started to jog over.

James stiffened. She really hoped he didn't have his finger on the trigger. She did not want to get shot.

Cassie braced herself for whatever would happen next. Alex wasn't giving any kind of message that he knew something was wrong. But he had to know. There was no way that her leaving with James, barefoot and in pants and a tank top, would be normal.

"Drop the gun."

Both Cassie and James jumped when Max's deep voice sounded behind them. Cassie whirled. Max had clamped his hand around James's wrist. She backed up from the two men and almost squealed when she ran into another solid form.

"It's okay." Alex wrapped his arm around her shoulders.

"Oh, God!" She whimpered and relaxed against him.

"I won't repeat myself again. Drop the gun."

James yelled and released his hold on the weapon, causing it to fall to the ground.

"You okay?" Max asked, raking her up and down with his gaze.

She nodded. Cassie wished she could throw herself into his arms and have him hold her. She needed to let him take care of James first. She never wanted to see her assistant again.

"Now…" Max gave his attention back to James. "You and I are going to have a little talk."

"Let me go! I wasn't doing anything!"

Max gripped James' shoulder with his free hand. "We have your buddies from the gallery."

James paled, but Cassie didn't have any sympathy for him. There was no telling what would have happened to her if James had delivered her to the Church. James might not believe she was a shifter, but if anyone else had suspected, she could have been in real trouble.

"I just wanted to help her. To help all of you! You don't know what kind of monsters you're dealing with!"

"Monsters?" Max growled.

"James thinks that the reason my art is so popular is because shifters keep buying my work. That is why the Church wanted to stop the show. They don't want shifters in town," Cassie told him. She prayed that Max understood the unspoken part of that sentence. If James didn't think her family were shifters, then hopefully they could get by without having to reveal themselves.

"I see," Max said. Anger was radiating off him, but he still sounded calm. "I think holding an innocent woman at gunpoint makes someone a monster. Not if someone has the gift to turn into an animal."

"You're wrong! Let me take you to my uncle. He'll show you how evil they are."

"I would love to meet this uncle," Alex spoke up.

Max nodded in agreement.

Cassie didn't agree. She would be happy to stay away from the man. She was relieved to hear that the men from the Church who were at the gallery had been caught, but what exactly were they going to do with them?

"Damn!" she yelled. "There are more men coming! They were going to burn my house down."

"We've got them, plus the ones watching Jacob's place."

Cassie spun and saw Jacob, Chase, Shawn and three other men joining them. She placed her palm over her racing heart. "Please, no more surprises. I can't handle it."

Max frowned and motioned his brother closer. After he pushed James toward Chase, he marched up to her side. "Are you sure you're all right?"

She moved from Alex and her brother stepped away to join the other men. "I'm okay. I just don't want anyone else sneaking up on me."

"Well, we have the two Council representatives bringing the men from the gallery over. We should probably go meet them at the main house, so they don't have to look for us," Alex stated.

She bobbed her head in agreement. "Alcohol." *There will be alcohol in the main house.* Cassie's legs were barely holding her up. If she didn't get in a chair soon, she'd fall over.

Max intertwined his fingers through hers and lifted her hand. He kissed her knuckles, smiling. "I'll get you whatever you want. First, inside where I can keep an eye on you."

"Okay," she agreed. She sure could get behind that idea. "I can't believe I was wrong about James." They began to follow behind her brothers and the shifters as they escorted the humans to the house.

"I understand. And I really do think he believes he is helping you. If that helps," Max said."

"It doesn't. He was going to burn down my place!"

Max stopped and Cassie found herself held tightly as Max dropped his mouth to hers. She opened to him and grasped at the back of his T-shirt to keep him close. The scent and flavor of him calmed her wolf. It was amazing how just his presence was helping. He pulled away and she was surprised by the stress lines on his forehead.

"I was so scared. Kurt and Clint called and said that they'd caught a couple of guys trying to break into the gallery and knew for sure James was involved, I just about lost it. Thank God for your brother. He managed to calm me down enough so I didn't barge into the studio and waited until the two of you came out."

Cassie cupped his face. "I was trying to figure out what to do."

"I know. And I knew that you'd be upset that James had turned on you."

"I am," she admitted. "But I also know that he doesn't understand. He's been surrounded by hatred. I wish he could see how much being a shifter is a gift."

"Maybe someday he will. Let's head up to the house. Kurt and Clint will help clean up this mess. They'll deal with the Church, so we can go on remaining hidden."

"I'm glad we weren't exposed. But I have to wonder how long it will last."

Max sighed. "Me, too. But we'll figure it out. Shawn won't let anything bad happen to the Pack. I bet he's already working on whatever needs to be done."

"I know Shawn will do what he can. What if it's not enough, though?" She didn't normally let her worries take over, but Cassie was finding it hard to accept such hate directed at her and all the shifters.

"It will be," he assured her.

"I'm glad this is over. But I have a feeling things aren't quite the same anymore. Not around here."

Max hugged her. "Yeah."

They walked quietly to the main house, entering though the back door. The low sound of voices reached her as she and Max strolled closer to the den. Cassie paused in the doorway and watched Alpha Shawn speak with James and several others. The two Council shifters stood glaring at the other group. Apparently not everything was going well.

Alex spotted them and tilted his head forward. Max pulled her out of sight until Alex joined them in the hall.

"James and a couple of the others want us to talk to his uncle. They seem determined to make us see the light about accepting the shifters. The other group from the gallery won't say a word. Kurt has a call in to the Council to see what exactly they want them to do next. Clint thinks they should go to the Church."

"But they can't!" Cassie exclaimed.

Alex shook his head. "We're pretty sure that someone from the Church would recognize them, so I agree. But they're right, too. We need to know more about this chapter. From what James is saying, his uncle is good friends with the senator who is trying to pass a law to make all shifters register."

"I still don't get that," Max said from beside her. "How would that help?"

"I don't know, but I don't like it. No one believes it'll pass. We worked with the government when all the shifters announced their presence, so we already have their support. Human and shifter leaders both agreed long ago that all shifters would be treated just like humans. I know the Shifter Coalition is involved in speaking with our government officials to make sure that nothing has changed, though."

Cassie groaned. "I wish they would all just leave us alone."

Alex patted her shoulder. "I don't think that will happen. There will always be someone who fears us because we're different."

"You're right. I'm just tired."

It was taking every bit of control Max had to keep from going into the living room and ripping James' throat out. If he could have transformed, Max was certain he'd have shifted with how angry he was.

Even at that moment he could feel the pull of his wolf.

Max had been in some serious situations. The missions he'd spent his entire life undertaking hadn't taxed him as much as seeing Cassie in danger. That fucker James had been standing there with his gun pointed at her back. How Alex had been so calm, Max would never know.

"I still need that drink," she whispered.

Shit. Max still had a job to do. Instead of following his Alpha's orders, Max wanted to take care of Cassie. That was the most important job he'd ever had. "And I said I'd get it for you." Max turned to Alex. "What are you going to do with them right now?"

"I had Kurt and Kyle take them to the stables," Alpha Shawn said as he stepped into the hall with them. "More guards are on the way. Just in case the Church sends someone after James and his cronies."

"Good idea," Alex said. "Come on." He urged Cassie into the living room. Max took her right to the couch before taking a seat with her.

"I'll grab the good stuff," Alex said.

Cassie cuddled into his side while their Alpha sat in the chair across from them. Shawn smiled at them.

"I didn't see this," Shawn waved his hand between them.

"Me, neither," Max said.

Cassie giggled. "Could we not discuss my love life with my brother in the room?"

"Please," Alex agreed.

Shawn grinned. "Sure."

"As much as you probably don't want to talk about James either, we need to know everything he told you," Alex ordered as he joined them. He had a glass bottle and four tumblers.

Cassie sighed so Max tightened his hold around her shoulders. "Fine." She received the first glass and had the contents downed before Alex was finished passing the drinks to the others. Max handed her his.

"Thanks," she murmured.

Max shrugged. If Cassie needed the entire bottle, that was fine with him.

"He didn't know I'm a shifter," she told them. "He kept saying that after his uncle explained things to me, I'd stop the shifters from buying my art."

"I can't believe I let him into our lives, our family," Alex said. He drained his glass. "I brought him into Cassie's life. This is my fault."

"No," Max and Cassie said at the same time.

"It's no one's fault but the humans who believe we're monsters," Shawn stated. "Even though they don't know better, we have to show them what we're really made of."

"Show them compassion," Max whispered. He could understand what his Alpha was saying. The humans feared them, but as a shifter community they had to prove they were also human.

"I hate them," Cassie said. "I've never hurt them. Not the way they hurt me — us."

"I know." Shawn leaned forward then placed his hand on her knee. "You're better than that, though."

"I don't want to be!" she shouted.

"Shh," Max comforted. "It's okay."

The tears he'd been expecting started to fall. Events had finally caught up with her and Cassie need to release the tension.

For the first time, the Alpha lost some of his composure. Max didn't know how Shawn could live with so many people relying on him all the time. The constant stress and worry he lived with had to be hard.

As Cassie cried herself out, the Alpha paced and Alex drank and Max just watched over them. Chase stepped into the room and stood at the entrance. Max started to shift Cassie away, but Chase merely shook his head. Max settled back down.

"Alpha?" Chase approached Shawn.

"The humans?" Shawn asked.

"Secure and under guard," Chase replied. "I've got the guards on shifts here and in town. Anyone not part of our Pack will be closely watched."

"Good." Shawn nodded. "No word from the Council?"

"No, Alpha," Chase responded. "I don't think it's likely they'll allow Kurt or Clint to go. Too big of a risk."

"I agree," Shawn said.

"Then we go." Alex stood.

Max agreed.

"No!" Cassie exclaimed. "It's not safe."

"If we go, there's a good chance that they'll figure out we're not human," Max said. "Is that a risk you're ready for?" He'd support his Alpha one hundred percent, always. That didn't mean he wasn't aware of the danger.

"That's what I'm struggling with," Shawn told him.

"Then I should go," Cassie said. "He'd expect me."

"No." Alex, Shawn, and Max all spoke.

"But—"

"No, Cassie." Alex leaned over and kissed her forehead. "I can't take the chance of anything happening to you."

"He's right," Shawn said. "I'll take Alex and Chase with me."

"The Alpha and both Betas?" Max asked. "How's that going to work? What if something happens to you three?"

"Without your successor named we can't all go," Chase said.

"I've chosen my successor," Shawn said. "The Council approved my choice as well."

"Really? Who?" Alex asked.

Alpha Shawn turned his gaze to Max. Alex and Chase both turned as well.

"What?" Max questioned.

"You," Shawn said. "I chose you."

Max had the sudden urge to look behind him to see who his Alpha was speaking to.

"That's brilliant." Chase grinned.

"No," Max blurted. "I can't be the Alpha!"

"Yes, you can," Shawn responded. "I've known since you were a teenager that you would replace me one day. Your years in the service taught you leadership and gave you confidence."

"I can't even shift," Max pointed out. This was crazy. Why would Shawn even consider naming Max as his successor?

"You always saw the fact that you couldn't shift as a weakness, when it's the opposite. The Council agrees. All I need is you to say yes."

Max looked from his Alpha to his brother. "I—"

"It doesn't have to be now," Shawn held up his hand. "I know we need to talk about this. Time to ask your questions. I wasn't going to bring this up until later."

"I can't believe this," Max admitted.

"It's something to think about," Cassie told him. She slipped her hand into his.

"Sure," Max replied. "Think about it."

"For now, I want to check on the humans," Shawn said. "We'll discuss a plan after."

"Peyton is bringing the boys over. I think we should all stay in the main house," Jacob said from the hall.

"Good idea," Alex replied.

"I need to grab a few things," Cassie said. "But we can stay here, too."

Max liked the way she included him.

"Max, will you take Cassie back to her place?" Shawn asked.

"Of course," Max agreed.

Cassie didn't let go of his hand during the walk back. Max was still reeling at what Shawn had said, so he remained quiet. He didn't want to think now. He suspected that his Alpha had wanted Max to feel pride in his decision, but all Max could think about was his failings. He couldn't lead a Pack—Max couldn't take care of himself most days.

"Stop!" Cassie demanded.

Max froze with his foot hovering over the bottom step to her house. "What?"

"I can see your emotions all over your face," Cassie said. "You don't think he should have chosen you."

He laughed, a low, bitter sound. "I know he made a mistake."

"Max. You might not believe it now, but there is a good reason why Shawn wants you to be his successor."

"What reason?"

Cassie placed her hand over his heart. "Because you'd do anything to protect the Pack. No one else is right for the job."

"I'm not like you," Max told her. "Not like any of them."

"Because you can't shift?" she asked. "So what, you can't change into a wolf. Is that really what makes us shifters special?"

"Of course it is," Max responded.

"Wrong." She gripped his hand before yanking him up the porch. Cassie pushed him into a chair before she knelt in front of him. "What makes us special is our community, our bonds. We're special because we have each other."

"And we can shift," Max said. "Or most can."

Cassie nodded. "Okay, that's very cool. One of the best things, but it doesn't matter how big someone's wolf form is. Or how fast they shift. The leadership, the Alphas, are so much more than all that."

"And you really think I have it in me?" Max knew he didn't.

"I believe it with all my heart," she replied. "And it's not just my life I'd willingly place in your hands. My brothers', Peyton's and my nephews' too. The ones that mean the most to me. I trust you to protect them."

"I... I still need to think about it," Max said. Was he seriously even considering saying yes? He gazed at Cassie, who seemed sure enough for him.

"That's smart," Cassie said. "Talk to Shawn and your brother. Hell, talk to me. Just give it time."

"I am so incredibly lucky," he murmured. "I will never understand what you see in me."

"Oh, Max," she crooned. "So much."

He'd had enough thinking, not knowing and questioning himself. Max leaned forward until he could press his lips against hers. Cassie hummed then climbed into his lap. As she ground down on his erection, Max grasped her hips while rocking up.

She tasted sweet like candy. He drank in her flavor, almost growing drunk from the connection that sparked between them.

He pulled back. "We should not do this outside here."

"But I want you," she argued. "Now."

Shit. Max had to do the right thing and get them both inside. He stood, using his shifter strength to pick her up easily. Okay, so maybe there was more to being a shifter than just transforming. Like being able to carry his lover into the house at an increased speed, Cassie chuckling in his ear the entire time.

"Where to?" he asked.

"My bedroom," she said. "I want you in my bed."

Well, he wasn't going to argue with that. Max stomped through the house until he laid her on her mattress. She propped herself onto her elbows as he went back and closed the door behind them. Even with the curtains shut tight, he could admire her from where he stood across the room.

"Take off your shirt," he ordered. As she complied, he did the same.

Cassie grinned back at him before he removed her bra.

Max licked his lips, wanting to taste the flawless skin she'd revealed. But first, she was wearing too many clothes. He ran his finger down the zipper of his jeans.

Cassie nodded then lifted her hips before removing her cotton pants and panties.

"Beautiful," he said. She was gloriously naked and obviously aroused.

"You're not so bad yourself."

Max bent over and untied his boots before shucking them and his socks. Only then could he shove his pants off. He straightened to find Cassie had crawled to the end of the bed.

He stroked his cock, bringing himself fully hard. "Whatcha want?" he teased.

"You." She crooked her finger at him. "Come closer."

"Sure." Max took two steps forward.

"Closer," she said.

Another step.

"You're still too far away," she complained.

"Sorry." Max walked in front of her until he could slide his fingers into her silky hair. He liked the way she kept her hair looking both sassy and hip, the color and shades bringing out the emotions in her eyes.

She was peering up at him with want and need.

"You want to suck me?" he asked.

Cassie nodded.

"Do it."

Cassie wrapped her hand around the base of his shaft before taking the tip into her mouth.

He closed his eyes and let his head fall back. Cassie sucked gently, playing with him.

Max tightened his grip on her hair then thrust deep. Cassie didn't pull back, but instead seemed to welcome every inch of him. Only the hand around his cock kept him from hitting the back of her throat.

"Yes." He groaned showing her his appreciation.

She bobbed her head in time with his hips. It wasn't long until Max was close to falling over the edge. He didn't want to come in her mouth, though. Max wanted to claim her from the instead out.

"Stop." He pulled back even when she attempted to chase him.

Max urged her onto her back with her legs over the side of the mattress. He ran the tip of his fingers up her thighs to find her pussy wet.

"In me," she pleaded. "Now."

One night he was going to spend every second tasting her and driving her crazy, but he needed to lose himself tonight. To just let go and feel.

He spread her thighs open before teasing his shaft between her slick folds.

Cassie pressed down, trying to take him inside.

Max grinned. He watched her as he began to fill her.

"Max!" Cassie arched her back as he slid inside.

The feeling of home and right flooded him. This was where he belonged. He might not know what the future held for him or the Pack, but in that moment, everything was perfect.

Chapter Nine

Nerves were getting the best of her and Cassie was seconds from freaking out. The gallery show was a success and everybody who was anybody was in attendance. She wanted to go back to her studio. Even better would be if she could convince Max to take her home and to bed.

The previous evening had been everything she had ever dreamed about.

Perfect, in every way. Until Max had woken screaming for his best friend.

Cassie hadn't known what to do except give him the space he said he wanted. Since he'd climbed out of bed, they hadn't had a moment alone. She wasn't going to get it anytime soon, either, with so many strangers around.

"How're you holding up?" Alex joined her where she was hiding along a back wall. He passed her a flute of champagne before taking a sip of his own.

"Fine," she responded. They both knew she was lying.

"Almost every piece has sold. The ones that haven't will be soon."

Cassie shrugged. At least she wasn't allowing the portraits of Max's unit to be sold off. They were promised to him. She wouldn't break her word. No matter how much the offers kept increasing.

Alex sighed. "I'm sorry about James."

She peered over to the wall that should have been holding James' work. Her assistant had been her friend, but now he sat in a jail cell for attempted arson, breaking and entering and attempted kidnapping. The Council had sent more representatives to deal with the Church. Alpha Shawn had kept his word to the Pack to keep them hidden. Cassie was relieved.

In the short time since the shifters had gone public, there been so much hate. She didn't want that directed at them. There was a reason she preferred to stay hidden away in the canyon. No one could hurt her or her family.

"Hey." Alex nudged her. "I lost you there for a second."

Cassie laughed. "Is it almost time to leave?"

"Another hour," Alex responded.

"Fine." Cassie finished off her glass. "Then get me another drink."

"I've got one right here." Alpha Shawn placed a flute in her free hand before taking her empty glass. "You looked like you needed it."

"Thanks, Alpha."

"I'm going to mingle some more," Alex told her. "One more hour."

"Yeah."

Her Alpha waited until Alex was across the room before moving shoulder to shoulder with her. "You look very pretty tonight."

Cassie glanced down at her simple black dress. The men wore suits and women dresses. She had also kicked off her heels within the first hour of the show. She probably looked ridiculous, especially surrounded by such elegant people. She appreciated her Alpha trying to make her feel better. "Thanks."

Shawn chuckled. "I mean it. Max hasn't been able to take his eyes off you."

She looked up and across the room, seeing Max's gaze on her. Cassie smiled. "He looks good, don't you think?" The dark circles under his eyes weren't as bad as when he'd first showed up and his face had more color. He'd always been fit, but there was just something about the way he carried himself now that showed confidence.

"He does," Shawn agreed. "I'd hoped that when he helped you it would remind him that he still has something to offer. It worked."

"Max still has a long road ahead of him," she murmured. "He might not be ready for what you're asking of him."

"He will be," Shawn stated. "When the time is right. He'll step up and protect the Pack."

"I know," she said. "I guess…"

"What? Tell me. I want to know. I value your opinion."

"I'm worried that it might be too much too soon," she confided. Cassie didn't want to tell Shawn about the nightmares or betray what Max had told her.

"If he doesn't get the push he needs, Max will lose himself in his past," Shawn said. "The things he's seen and witnessed are enough to destroy any man. I don't want to lose him. I want him to fight."

Cassie agreed.

"He's already started," Shawn said. "Now we just need to make sure we're there for him when he needs it."

Across the room, Chase bumped Max and Max smiled wide. The brothers loved each other. That much was obvious, but it hadn't been enough to make Max happy. She hoped that she'd be able to add a little something to his life to help Max heal. To keep him with family. "What should I do?"

"Listen," Shawn advised. "Let him talk about the men who were his brothers. Allow him to share stories. You're keeping them alive for him." Shawn nodded toward the series she'd painted of Max's unit. "That's the best gift you could have given him."

Cassie would paint him a hundred portraits if that helped Max. Maybe she could even see a picture of how they really looked, in addition to the animal forms she'd created of them based on how Max described each of his friends. "Okay."

"I better go check in with the security detail," Shawn said. "I don't foresee any problems with the Council reps here, but better safe than sorry."

"Thanks for checking on me," she said.

Shawn kissed her cheek. "Always."

After her Alpha left her, Cassie searched out Max again. He was slowly making his way toward her but kept getting stopped by the members of the Pack that were in attendance. He seemed surprised each time one of the ladies would kiss his cheek or the men shake his hand.

Cassie had always considered Max and his family an important part of the Pack. It broke her heart that Max hadn't felt a part of them. Finally, after several long minutes, Max made it to her side.

"Your brother said I could sneak you away," he whispered to her.

"Really?" Cassie straightened up. That was the best news she'd heard all night.

"Come on." He urged her toward the back. "Where are your shoes?"

Cassie looked around but couldn't remember where she'd left the dreadful heels. She shrugged.

Max's chuckled was warm. "That's all right." He continued to guide her to where she knew the back door was. The store room they walked through was cool, dark and organized. That had been James' doing. Now they'd have to find someone else.

At the exit, Max pushed open the door before lifting her up. Cassie threw her arm around his neck as he held her under her legs as well.

"I could get used to this," she teased.

"Baby, I'll carry you anywhere you want to go."

And just like that, Cassie saw their entire future. Max carrying her over the threshold after marriage, him holding a baby and even the two of them rocking on the porch, watching the sun set behind the canyon.

If she got a choice, she'd make the dreams a reality.

But she had to take her time.

Max was still healing and he probably wasn't ready for her to inform him that she was already planning the next sixty to eighty years together.

The black SUV they'd driven in sat close to the back door. Cassie was disappointed the walk wasn't longer. She really enjoyed being in his arms.

He clicked the key fob to unlock the passenger door before settling her inside.

Cassie grabbed hold of Max's face then drew his lips to hers. "I'm glad you were there with me tonight," she told him once she pulled away.

"I enjoyed the show. It's nice to see all your hard work being appreciated."

She nodded. It was. After her art was sold, Cassie always imagined where each piece ended up. In a surprising twist, Kurt Moore, one of the Council reps, had confessed he had one of her wolf landscape scenes over his bed. He and his mate had recently moved in together and both had decided to leave it where it was.

Cassie was proud she could touch someone that strongly.

"There's a couple more nights," she told him. "Opening night is the only time I have to attend, but the show will continue for three more evenings. After that, we'll deliver your portraits back to you."

Max stepped back, still caught by the door, as he peered at her. "I heard what everyone was saying. You had offers on the series."

"I'm not selling."

"I can't let you give up the money for me," he responded. "Maybe—"

"No. Those are yours."

"I don't even have a place to hang them," he said.

"Yes, you do." Cassie grinned.

Max blinked at her. "You mean…"

"That you don't have to leave now that the Church is stopped?"

He nodded.

"I like having you around," she told him. "If you want to go back to Chase's house or stay with the Alpha, I'll keep them safe for you."

"I don't know what to do about the Alpha's offer," he confided.

"I know."

Max patted her legs before carefully closing the door. As he walked in front of the vehicle, she watched him. The way he darted his gaze around them to make sure no one was near. Even though the Council was taking care of the threat, Max was still ensuring her safety.

After he climbed inside behind the wheel, she leaned over and kissed his cheek. "Thank you."

"I won't let anything happen to you," Max stated.

"I have no worries with you around," she replied.

"Then let me get you home." He started the SUV.

"You'll have to carry me inside."

"Oh, don't you worry about it," Max said. "I know exactly where I want to put you."

Cassie shuddered at the promise that dripped from his tone. She couldn't get wait to get back to her house.

The ride was quiet, but Cassie didn't mind. Max glanced all around them as he drove. He was still in protection mode. Once they were behind her locked doors with the alarm system, she'd be able to distract him from all his worries.

She pressed her forehead to the side glass as the scenery passed by quickly. It was only about a twenty-minute drive to her property and she knew the route well.

Too soon, she felt the vehicle slow down.

Cassie sat up. "What's wrong?"

"Do you have your cell?"

"No, I didn't bring it."

Max shoved his into her hand. "Call the Alpha."

"What's going on?" She peered through the windshield but all she could see were lights from oncoming vehicles. Several. And one vehicle was in their lane heading right toward them. Cassie dialed Shawn's cell phone number.

"Put it on speaker," Max ordered.

She complied just as Shawn answered.

"Max?" Shawn barked.

"Mile marker fifty-three," Max said.

"On my way," Shawn responded. "Stay safe."

"Hurry," Max demanded.

Through the phone, she could hear Shawn issuing orders including one to call Kurt or Clint.

They were barely creeping along now. Nowhere near the seventy-five miles per hour speed limit.

"Max!" Her voice shook as fear flooded her.

"It's going to be okay." He looked at her. "If I say run, I want you out of that door and on the move. Run until you get to a safe place, then shift."

"What about you?" Cassie did not want to leave Max behind.

"I'll be fine," he said. "I promise."

She gripped his hand. "You have to be. I need you."

Max pulled over off to the side. The other vehicles were still headed toward them. Maybe it was just regular drivers. Maybe there was no threat.

Not that she believed that.

It was dark and she could feel in her bones they were in trouble.

Max put the SUV in Park before turning to her. "Do whatever I say. Get to your house and lock yourself inside. I'll meet you there."

"Swear!" she demanded. "Swear that you'll be right behind me."

He kissed her quickly. "I swear."

"Okay." She took deep breaths and peered out of the window. There was nothing around. Just low, dead grass. Not even a place to hide. About five hundred yards away, there were some large boulders and jagged rocks. She could make it there. Cassie was fast. She'd have an advantage over any humans. Unless they had guns. Yeah, the humans could just shoot her and Max, leaving their bodies before Shawn reached them. "Oh God." She bent over and wrapped her arms around her stomach. She couldn't do this. Cassie wasn't made for all this fucking drama.

"No!" Max gripped her head and dragged her up. "You will not give up on me. You are going to do exactly as I say. We're going to be fine."

Cassie couldn't control the shaking in her hands. She wrapped her palms around her knees and squeezed.

"After this we're going to lock ourselves in your house for days. I'm going to make love to you over and over. We'll only get out of bed to shower and eat. No, fuck that — we can eat in bed."

She laughed. "That sounds good."

"They're here," he said. He let go of her and straightened in the seat.

There were three dark vehicles blocking them from moving forward. From the middle SUV, the driver's door opened and a man stepped out. Both she and Max leaned forward but Cassie didn't recognize the stranger.

"We just want to talk!" the stranger shouted.

Max rolled his window down. "Then talk."

"There's been a misunderstanding," the man said. "And my nephew is paying the price."

Cassie gasped. "It has to be James' uncle."

"Yeah," Max murmured. "That's my guess."

"You'd have to contact the police," Max yelled. "We have nothing to do with that."

"It's already being done," the man replied. "But my nephew is upset. He didn't mean to scare Ms. Wilson. He'd like me to talk with Ms. Wilson. To allow her to hear what she needs to."

"There's nothing that she needs to hear from the people who tried to burn down her house and kidnap her," Max argued.

"Please," the man said. "Just talk."

Max cracked open the door.

"What are you doing?" Cassie asked in a panic. Max should not be getting out of the SUV.

"Buying us some time," Max replied. "Just stay next to me."

He slipped out of the vehicle before helping her over the console and into the driver's seat. Cassie did not want to get out, but she'd promised she'd listen to him.

Max helped her down but moved his body to block hers.

"Ms. Wilson."

"Who… What do I call you?" she asked.

"You may call him Jeremiah," the stranger replied. "It is my Church name."

"Jeremiah," she repeated. "I want to go home. Please let us pass."

"I wish I could, young lady," Jeremiah responded. "It's not safe for you there. You're trusting the wrong people. Or things."

"We just want to stay on our property and live our lives," Cassie said.

"My nephew thinks the world of you. I offered to show you the light," Jeremiah told her. "Come with me." He held out his hand.

Cassie had no desire to go near the man. He repulsed her.

"She's not going anywhere with you," Max said.

"I thought you'd say that," Jeremiah said. He pulled out a black gun at the same time as the doors of other the vehicles opened.

The strangers spread out. Eleven men joined Jeremiah.

"I must insist Ms. Wilson comes with me, though. She'll tell the police that James' involvement was just a mistake. My nephew will be released. Then we will educate her on what she's been associating with." Jeremiah waved the gun. "Now, come here, Ms. Wilson."

"Get ready to run," Max whispered.

"Okay." Cassie took a few steps back. She could dart around the SUV then run full out. She'd have to trust Max to keep his word.

"I don't have all night," Jeremiah shouted. "Now, Ms. Wilson."

Cassie was seconds from making a break for it when a long, loud howl broke through the silence.

The humans yelled before pulling out more weapons.

"Hurry," Jeremiah ordered. "Grab the girl and let's get out of here."

One of the men started toward her. Max pushed Cassie back before growling at the humans.

"He's one of the monsters!" Jeremiah called. "Take him out."

Cassie hit the ground when she heard the first bullet. She rolled and rolled until she was under the SUV and on the other side. She started to scream when her momentum was stopped by a body.

"Shh," Alex covered her mouth with his hand.

"Oomph." She sagged against her brother.

There were more growls, the sound echoing around them. Coming up from the side of the road were dozens of wolves. Wolf shifters. Her Pack. They were coming to help.

She pushed Alex's hand off. "Max! I think he was shot."

"He'll be fine," Alex told her. "Shawn is with him. Now, let's get you out of here."

Cassie tried to stand, but her legs were shaking and she was sick to her stomach. The events from earlier still had her reeling.

"Come on, I'll help you." Alex kept one arm around her waist as he led her to a dark BMW that she hadn't noticed parked behind her.

She tried to look over her shoulder to where Max was but couldn't see anything. Alex bundled her into the passenger side before he raced around the front. Before she even had his seat belt on, he was backing up fast.

"Where are we going?" she asked.

"Home," he replied. "Just taking the long way."

"Home," she repeated. "I want to go home."

Max's arm burned where the bullet had grazed him. If it hadn't been for Kurt, Clint and a couple of other guards coming out of the dark and jumping the humans, he'd be dead for sure. Being killed would had have him breaking his promise to Cassie. He would return to her.

"You okay?" Shawn asked, joining him.

"Fine." He rotated his shoulder. It was just a flesh wound and he'd had worse. "Where's Cassie?"

"Alex took her home," Shawn said. "She doesn't need to be involved in this."

"Thanks." He turned at a sound close to him to see Kurt Moore approaching. "Hey, man, everything good?"

"The cops are on their way," Kurt said. "These men are human, so we have no jurisdiction to hold them."

"They shot my man," Shawn said with a growl.

Kurt started to examine Max. "Are you okay? Where's the wound?"

"I'm fine." Max shrugged Kurt off him. "Just a scrape."

"Of course," Kurt stated. "We'll get things handled here. Why don't you head back to the ranch? I'll give the cops your number, so they can schedule an interview."

"I'm not going to argue with that," Max responded. He was tired. And all Max wanted was to see that Cassie was safe.

"I'll give you a lift," Shawn offered.

"Thanks, Alpha." Max strolled to the same passenger seat that he'd helped Cassie into earlier. When she hadn't had shoes on. Jeez, he'd barely gotten them out of there alive. He'd had many guns pointed at him but never had he felt fear like when Cassie had been in the line of fire.

"There's a first-aid kit in the back seat," Shawn told him. "You should take care of that wound before Cassie sees it."

"Good idea." Max reached behind the seat and dug around until his hand landed on a smooth box. He removed his suit jacket and tossed it into the back. He took the sleeve of his shirt and ripped the seam. Shifter strength sure did come in handy.

With his uninjured arm, he opened the case and removed what he needed. They bumped along a dirt road which made his arm ache, but Max clenched his teeth and endured. He wouldn't show weakness in front of his Alpha.

He did the best job he could cleaning the wound then applying a thick layer of cream. They were just entering the Wilson property when he attempted to bandage himself.

"Leave it," Shawn ordered. "I'll do it when we park."

Max nodded before pulling out the bandages he wanted.

Shawn pulled up in front of Cassie's house. He turned the ignition off then flicked on the interior lights. "Let me see."

Max passed him the bandages before sticking out his upper arm. There was some meat missing but Max would make a full recovery.

"This might sting a bit," Shawn said before he pressed the bandage against his arm.

Max pressed his lips together but didn't utter a sound.

"There that should do it. And just in time." He motioned to the front of Cassie's house. "Someone's waiting on you."

"Thanks, Alpha," Max repeated then climbed out of the SUV.

Cassie walked down the steps. At least she had flip flops on. He opened his arms and she launched herself the rest of the way. Max caught her and held her close to his body.

The sound of Shawn backing away barely registered as he kissed her with all the passion he held inside.

"You kept your promise," she whispered, pulling away.

"Always."

He kissed her again as he walked up the steps. Cassie wrapped her legs around his waist, allowing him to carry her. Just like he'd planned all along. It had taken him longer than he'd wanted to get her home and safe.

The front door was already open for him to stroll through. As he locked it and set the alarm, Cassie nibbled on his neck. Holy shit, he was so fucking horny. Max needed Cassie like never before.

"Take me to bed," Cassie whispered. "You promised that we'd only leave my bed to shower."

He had said that. "And I've already shown I keep my promises."

"Please."

Max stopped at the fridge and leaned down. "Grab a couple of bottles of water. We're going to need them."

Cassie laughed. "You don't really have to carry me everywhere."

"But I do," Max told her. "You will not be walking anytime soon. I'll even carry you to the shower."

"I guess it's a good thing that I already turned the sheets down on the bed."

It was indeed. Max strode down the hall and right into her bedroom. Not only had she folded the sheets back, but she had also lit candles, placing them all around the room.

"It's beautiful," he said. "Just like you." Max gently placed her on the mattress.

"Make love to me. Just like you said you would."

"Wait." He held up his finger then walked over to the stereo in the corner. Max hadn't owned anything other than his iPhone for music in years. But as he pressed the Power button, smooth jazz came though the speakers in the corner of her bedroom ceiling.

"Oh nice," she praised.

Max strolled back to the bed to stand over her. "Now let's see about me keeping my word to you." He slowly undressed her before taking the time to bare himself. Max tossed the clothing onto the floor, not really caring where it landed. They could clean up later. Much later.

Once he was naked, he climbed onto the bed, between her legs.

Cassie arched into his touch when he cupped her breasts. "I love the feel of your hands on me."

"Almost as much as I love touching you," he replied.

"Touch me more," she demanded.

Max skimmed his hands up her legs while bending to kiss her neck. Cassie gasped and clutched at him. Even as she dug her nails into his back, he didn't raise her head. He licked and teased both of her nipples before trailing his tongue down to her belly button.

He ignored her whimpering and pleas. This part was all for him.

She tasted sweet, like apples and candy. The sounds coming from her mouth were even more satisfying, as he savored every sip taken from her skin.

"Mine," he murmured. Max ran a finger through her slick folds until he thrust one digit into her pussy.

Cassie moaned, then lifted her hips, shoving his digit further inside. He played with her clit with his tongue while taking her over the first crest of orgasm. Max didn't stop until she was begging him.

"Please, Max!"

He moved up to his knees then wrapped his hand around his cock and stroked. *Fuck.* He was already so close to coming.

Apparently tired of waiting for him, Cassie reached up and tugged him down on top of her. Max grunted from the impact then lifted enough to drag his cock over Cassie's stomach. He trailed precum onto her soft skin.

"I know you want me," she murmured.

Max gripped his shaft before positioning the tip at her entrance. She looked up at him and he held her gaze as he plunged deep.

Cassie bowed up, but that just let him slide in even farther.

"Yes!" she shouted.

He withdrew before thrusting again and again. Max kept a steady pace. The exhaustion he'd felt earlier was gone and the only thing that mattered was showing Cassie how much she meant to him. That he loved her.

It might be too soon to declare what he saw as his future, but Max still imagined it.

He'd never allow Cassie to doubt how much he needed her, wanted her. She'd always know she was loved.

Max rocked in and out of her until Cassie was clawing at his back and shouting with her second climax. He rode her through her body tightening and clamping down on his cock. Finally, he couldn't take it anymore and yelled as he came.

"Fuck!" Max didn't think he'd ever released so much seed before. He barely managed to pull out before he collapsed down beside her.

"That was great," she praised.

"Give me ten minutes and it'll be time for round two."

Cassie patted his naked ass. "Whatever you say, dear."

Max closed his eyes before he yanked Cassie closer. She cuddled up to his side then laid her head on his chest. He slid his fingers through her hair. This was how they belonged. Forever.

It was hot. So fucking hot. Max couldn't wait until he was back home, grilling out and drinking a cold beer. Evan would get drunk and have to sleep on his couch, but Max really didn't mind. He missed Chase, and Evan was like a brother as well. Of course, Evan wasn't the same as Chase since he couldn't shift and run under the full moon. A brother was still a brother.

"I need a stiff drink," Evan bitched.

"One double shot coming right up," Max said with a chuckle. He tossed his canteen to his best friend. "Drink up."

Evan chugged the water then wiped his mouth with the back of his hand. "Doesn't taste like any double I've ever had."

"It washes the sand down anyway," Max quipped. He wanted to leave this fucked-up country and never come back. They'd been out for over forty-eight hours with no idea when they'd get the final push to begin their mission.

Max blinked the dirt from his eyes. They ached, from tiredness to wariness.

He opened them back up and he was standing in the middle of the canyon. The full moon illuminated the same spot that Cassie had shared with him. But instead of the woman he loved, his best friend stood peering back at him.

"Evan," he whispered. Max didn't know why. It just felt as if he spoke too loudly, Evan would leave him again.

"So many secrets," Evan responded. He shook his head even as he smiled. "I always knew there was something special about you."

"I'm sorry I never told you. I was going to, after our last mission." A tear escaped. "But you never came home."

"Oh, but I did, old friend."

Max swiped at his tears. "I failed you."

"No, I failed you." Evan always did love to argue.

"I let you die!" His voice echoed around the empty canyon walls.

"I died, yes, but you're not alone."

"I need you by my side," Max confided. "I miss you."

"I miss you, too, brother. But you have a chance at something wonderful."

The scenery changed again.

Max was in bed with Cassie with her practically lying on top of him. His fingers were still buried in her hair as he held her as close as he could.

"She's beautiful, perfect for you," Evan stood beside the bed. "I always knew when you fell in love, it'd be with a strong woman."

"I love her," he confessed.

"Of course you do. So why are you doubting your abilities? Why haven't you answered your Alpha?"

"I'm not worthy of his offer. The Pack will not follow a non-shifting shifter."

"I think you underestimate them. They'll follow you because you're the right person for the job. You'll protect them in this time of chaos."

"And if I fail them like I did you?" Max asked. It was the question that was haunting him.

"The only way to fail is by not trying," Evan replied. "You know this."

Max nodded. He did. Their missions were never guaranteed. It took the entire team, each one a master at their *craft, to survive. "I need people I can trust." Just like those in his old unit.*

"It's a good thing you already have that. Your brother, her brothers, the guards who've followed our lead so far. All you must do is accept. Everything will fall into place."

"I hope you're right."

Evan flashed him that same cocky grin Max knew so well. "I'm always right."

"I'm sorry," Max whispered. "I'm so fucking sorry."

"You have to stop punishing yourself. Embrace this opportunity."

Max gasped as he sat up in bed. He peered around the room, but of course Evan wasn't there. It had only been another nightmare, or dream. He wasn't used to this peaceful feeling after dreaming about his unit or best friend. Was it a sign? Could Max be ready to finally move on with his life? Evan had come to him and given his blessing so it sure as hell seemed as if he needed to figure his shit out once and for all.

He knew it hadn't really been Evan talking to him, but Max still believed he had his best friend's blessing to stop living in the past. Max needed to embrace his future.

Not wanting to wake Cassie, Max slipped his arm out from under her. He rolled out of bed gently before tugging the comforter over her.

Cassie made a small sound of protest before she turned onto her stomach. She wiggled around until she dug her face into his pillow. He smiled before he left, closing the door behind him.

The studio door was right there and all Cassie's work was currently at the gallery.

Max pushed the door open. The space seemed so much bigger without the numerous canvasses lined up against the wall. He strolled over to the balcony, stopping only to turn off the alarm from his phone, before pulling open both doors.

The night air was cool and a soft breeze ruffled his hair as he stepped into the darkness. Lights shone out from Alex's house and it reminded him that he had the people he needed to talk to. But first he would have to accept the new position.

The Alpha prodigy or some shit like that. The successor. The future Alpha.

All those titles sounded odd and unbelievable.

Max wasn't ready, but he'd make damn certain that when the time came, he was the best fucking Alpha anyone had ever seen.

"I find my lover standing outside, naked, and I don't know if I want to jump you or paint you."

Max whirled around to lean against the balcony. "Why don't you do both?"

Cassie chuckled. She walked over, just as naked as him, to kiss him deeply.

"Mmm," he murmured. Max slipped his hands down her back.

She pulled back and it almost took his breath away, she was so stunning. "What are you doing out here?"

"Just thinking." He turned so she was in front of him with him warming her from behind. The entire Wilson ranch was spread out before them.

"About what?"

"My future, our future," he replied. Cassie stiffened, but he nuzzled her neck. "All good, I promise."

"You want to talk about it?"

"I'm going to allow Shawn to train me as the future Alpha," he confided.

"Max! That's great." She tried to turn around, but he held her in place. "Just listen."

"Okay." She laid her head back on his chest.

"I'm going to tell Shawn that I accept until he finds someone else, changes his mind or I'm convinced I can do the job."

"You can."

"Thanks." He chuckled. "I appreciate the vote of confidence."

"I'll always believe in you."

"In the meantime, we still need to talk about us," he said.

"Us?" she repeated. "I thought we'd already decided."

This time it was Max making her spin around, so he could see her face. "I want more."

"More?"

"I don't just want to see if we can work out. I want us to," Max said. It was time to put all his cards on the table. If he scared her away, he'd give her space, while making sure she knew he meant every word.

"What are you saying?" she questioned. "Be specific."

"I don't want to leave," Max said. "I wish for my paintings to hang on the walls here. Where I can look at them every day."

"You'll stay here with me?" she asked in excitement.

"If you'll have me."

"Yes!" Cassie kissed him. "Yes!"

"Fair warning," Max told her. "I can be a pain in the ass before my coffee."

"I can be a pain in the ass all the time," she retorted.

Max laughed. "I can live with that."

"Me, too."

He kissed her again, this time lifting her so he could take her back to bed. Max had made a promise to make love to her for forty-eight hours. It was time he got started.

Chapter Ten

Max grunted as he rolled away from his Alpha. The training that he was enduring wasn't just mental or social. He also had to tap into his wolf's dominant fighting urges to protect the Pack.

It turned out that Max had the ability to draw from his wolf even more than he'd imagined. Shawn had explained that as he came to accept his position, not only would his connection with his wolf be stronger, but with the territory as well.

He slowly rose to his feet before he faced off against his Alpha again. Max nodded before taking his fighting stance again. This time he closed his eyes then breathed deeply. Someone had cut the lawn recently—Max smelled the moist soil beneath the short blades of grass. If he could just connect with the land...

"You're still holding back," Shawn said. "You have to embrace your strengths."

"I am," he argued. "I have been," He was stronger, faster and more determined. There was still something missing though.

"More," Shawn demanded. "Use more of your instincts."

Sweat dripped from his forehead and he wiped it away. He would not stop before his Alpha. "Bring it."

With his eyes still closed he still felt the air around him move as Shawn attacked. Max dodged the first blow then ducked a second. He was on the defense and had to turn things around. He dropped to his knees before lunging at his Alpha. He caught Shawn around the waist and took him down.

Max grinned down at his Alpha. "Like that?"

"Not bad," Shawn said. "There's just one more thing."

"What?" He went flying through the air, only to land on his back again. His breath whooshed out of him. Max groaned.

Shawn stood over him and grinned. "Again?" He offered his hand to Max to help him up.

Max allowed Shawn to pull him to his feet.

"How about you take a break from kicking my boyfriend's ass and have a drink?" Cassie called.

Max straightened and turned to find Cassie sitting on the porch. He'd been so focused on the Alpha he hadn't realized she'd come out of her studio. She'd been locked inside for a few days, starting a new series. Cassie wouldn't tell him what she was working on, but he was certain it would be fabulous.

"How long have you been sitting there?" he asked.

Shawn laughed. "Enough to witness your last two failures."

Max looked over at him. Of course, Shawn had known she was there. He'd had years of practice at this. Before he'd started his training, Max had believed the hardest part was getting the Pack to accept him. He now realized that there was so much more to leading then settling feuds between two Pack members. He had so much to learn. Max growled low in the back of his throat with frustration.

"Don't be too hard on yourself," Shawn said, slapping him on the back. "You're doing better than I did at three days."

"Really?"

Shawn nodded. "Yes."

That made him feel better.

"Of course, I was thirteen."

Max laughed. His Alpha had a wicked sense of humor that Max hadn't known about. Not only was he being trained, but he also was learning more about his Alpha. If possible, he not only respected the man more but liked him more as well.

"I have ice water," Cassie teased. She picked up one of the bottles and waved it at him.

Oh yeah, Max so wanted a drink of that. He strolled forward with Shawn on his heels. Cassie handed him the bottle before passing one over to Shawn. Max took a chair next to Cassie and leaned back. It was hot out even though the sun had barely been up for a couple of hours. A beer would be better but drinking before eight in the morning wasn't a good idea.

"Taking a break?" Chase questioned. He walked up the steps of the porch before leaning back against the rail.

Max grinned at his brother. "We've been up for hours. Did you just crawl your ass out of bed?"

Chase chuckled. "I'll have you know I opened the diner this morning."

"And you didn't bring us any pie?" Max complained. "That's just not right."

"Sorry." Chase held his hands up. "All out."

"Damn."

"What brings you by?" Shawn asked. "Not that I'm not happy to see you. But, like Max said, you didn't even bring us pie."

Chase laughed. "One-track minds."

"Well," Max said with a shrug, "training's hard."

"Come by for lunch," Chase offered. "All of you, I'll make sure to have a fresh pie for you."

Max exchanged a look his Alpha. It was time he went into town more often. Max was going to have to bond with his pack mates. "Sounds good."

Chase appeared surprised the grinned. "I did have a reason for coming over."

"What's wrong?" Max asked.

"There might be trouble in Lubbock," Chase told him. "Reports of the Church gearing up for another demonstration have reached the Council. They want to know if we have any people there."

Shawn glanced over at Max. "It's time for you to learn the least fun part of this job. How to keep the Pack safe."

"We have Pack there?" Max asked.

"Yes," Shawn answered. "A lot of the Pack attend the university there. Some of the parents moved to be closer to them. It's become more common in the last several years. We're funding as many of our young people that want to get a higher education."

Max had assumed that most of the Pack had stayed around the canyon. He should have asked more questions, gotten to know his Pack mates better. "That's great. Paying for the kids' college."

"It's a different world than when we were growing up," Chase said. "The kids don't want to stay around here and just live with the Pack. They want to travel, work and see things."

Max could understand that. He'd joined the military and had gotten to see places most people didn't. That was what he had wanted. He could really appreciate the fact that Shawn was making it possible for the kids in the Pack to grow and have real futures. "I... I like that."

"But if the Church is there we need to help them," Chase said. "If one of our Pack is outed it could mean trouble for all of us."

"What do we need to do?" Max asked.

"Get word to our people in Lubbock," Shawn said. "Maybe even send up some extra security. I'd prefer not to disrupt their lives if possible."

"I'll get it done," Chase promised. "I have a couple guards who wouldn't mind going up."

"I want to go," Max said. "We need to help them."

"I'll ask if anyone is willing is to return to the Pack. If they need help getting out, we'll send people. Between that and the extra guards, they should be fine."

"I should go," Max argued. This would be his first mission to help the people he'd eventually lead.

Shawn sighed. "That's your instincts talking, but now I need you to use your human intelligence. We're not out—it's important that we continue to protect the Pack here as well. With the recent brush up here your face is too recognizable."

"Shit." Max rose and began to pace. This was a difficult decision. He understood what his Alpha was saying, but that didn't mean he liked it. He was a man of action.

His path was blocked by Shawn stepping in front of him. "This is part of managing the Pack. Doing what is best for everyone."

"There hasn't been reports of any missing Pack or threats," Chase said. "This is more of a warning that with Jeremiah in custody in Lubbock, the Church is rallying there. We have no proof that any of us are in danger. It might be a peaceful protest."

Max snorted. The Church for Humanity never did anything peaceful. He didn't believe for a second that now would be any different.

"I just thought you both should know," Chase said. "For us to get ahead of this."

"You did well," Shawn said. "The more information we have, the better."

"Alex is waiting up at the main house," Chase responded. "Do you want to fill him in?"

"Yes." Max held his hand out to Cassie. "Coming?"

"Sure." Cassie walked beside him as Shawn and Chase led the way. "You okay?" she asked quietly.

"Yeah," Max responded. "I've been focusing on the physical part of being an Alpha, how to connect socially to the Pack. I hadn't really thought about the tough decisions that have to be made."

"You're doing a good job," Cassie whispered. "Shawn would tell you if you weren't."

"I feel like I'm thirteen again. Nothing I do seems to be enough. I'm awkward and slow."

Cassie laughed. "You're hot as hell, rolling around in the grass. I couldn't concentrate because you were so distracting."

"I'll take that as a compliment." He linked his fingers with hers as they walked up the deck steps leading to the glass door. It was open with Shawn, Chase and Alex already inside.

"Hey," Alex greeted.

"Good morning," Max said. "Sorry to interrupt you so early."

Alex waved his words away. "That's what I'm here for."

"What should we do first?" Max asked.

"I'll make coffee," Cassie offered. She gave him a quick kiss on the cheek before walking out of the room.

Max watched her go before he turned to his Alpha. "I'm not certain how worried I should be."

Shawn shook his head. "Me, neither. The Church was delivered a big blow here. That makes them dangerous."

"Yeah," Max agreed. "A cornered animal is always more dangerous. The Church has been proven to be nothing but animals."

"They won't be able to get their people out of jail," Chase said.

Max strolled to the patio door and peered out of the large sliding glass door. The quietness of the territory gave him peace, but for how long? By continuing this path, he'd have to deal with mornings like this often.

"You're doubting yourself," Shawn said from behind him.

Max didn't bother to turn around. "You really think I'm strong enough for this?"

"I know you are," Shawn stated firmly.

"But how?"

"Your first instinct is to go and protect your Pack. Unable to do that, you're struggling with the many options, outcomes and possibilities. Now it's time to figure out the solution."

"I just hope I don't screw this up and someone gets hurt," Max said.

"I'm by your side. We'll do this together," Shawn said.

Max closed his eyes and prayed for the safety of his Pack in Lubbock. "First let's get the guards headed that way? No pint in wasting time."

Shawn patted his shoulder. "Exactly." He turned to Chase. "Make the call."

Chase nodded before pulling out his phone. He walked to the other side of the room as he began to talk.

"What next?" Max questioned.

"Alex, why don't you get us a list of everyone who is living up in Lubbock," Shawn said. "If we work together we'll get the calls done faster. Have our people headed home and safe."

"You got it," Alex hurried over to his laptop.

"I know it's not what you want to be doing but it's the right decision. For now," Shawn told him.

"For now?" Max asked.

"Things can change quickly," Shawn advised. "We'll move ahead with this plan while making sure there is a backup strategy."

"Always be prepared," Max stated.

"That's right."

Max looked over his shoulder at his Alpha. Shawn was calm and collected. How was Shawn managing to keep it together? Max felt like he was about to crumble with all the stress and possible outcomes from the new threat.

"You need to give yourself a break," Shawn ordered. "Trust in the people who you've chosen to be by your side."

At that moment Cassie walked in carrying a tray with coffee mugs and a full pot.

"And here's your biggest supporter now," Shawn whispered.

Max rushed to Cassie and took the heavy tray from her hands. She smiled at him before Max turned and walked to set the refreshments on the coffee table.

"I got the names and numbers," Alex held up a list he'd printed from his laptop.

"Let's get started," Max suggested. "I'll feel much better once I know our people are safe from the Church."

Cassie and Max sat beside each other on the couch as Alex passed them both a page of Pack members' information.

He slid his finger over his phone's home screen. He was damn well going to protect his people.

* * * *

Cassie stretched her arms over her head. After working all morning contacting members of the Pack in Lubbock she'd gone to her studio to continue working on her newest series. One that she wasn't ready to tell anyone else about. Not even Max.

Or at least she hadn't until she'd figured out exactly where she was headed with this new work. Now in front of her was the portraits of her Alpha and the second one of the future Alpha.

The background for both was inside the canyon. The two men stood tall surrounded by their territory.

Behind Shawn were three male wolves and three females. His inner circle. The chosen few that would give their lives for the Alpha.

Max's portrait was different though. Cassie wasn't sure why she saw Max differently from Shawn. Max also had three male wolves and three females but instead of behind him, Max's inner circle were spread out by his side.

When she'd picked up her paintbrush she'd had no idea what inspiration would take her over. Now she grinned, thrilled with the outline of what would be an awesome series. She couldn't wait to show Max.

Cassie placed her brush inside the jar she used to clean them before turning to the door. She rushed forward and yanked the door open, practically running straight into Max.

"Shit!" she exclaimed.

Max caught her by the shoulders to keep her from bumping into him. "Hey."

"Sorry." She brushed her hair off her forehead. "I wasn't expecting you to be there."

He chuckled. "I was just coming to ask if you felt like going to the diner. We didn't make it for lunch."

"Mmm, pie!"

"Yeah," Max agreed. "After dinner, though. You need a good meal before you have dessert."

She slid her arms around him. "Dessert. I like the sound of that." Cassie lifted herself up to the tips of her toes. "Let's have dessert first. And I'm not talking about pie."

Max licked his lips before lowering his head. "Nope, dinner first."

"Damn." She smacked his chest. "You're mean."

"I'm just trying to take care of my girl."

Oh hell, when Max said things like that Cassie wanted to pull him into bed and never let him leave. "I have something to show you first." She grabbed his hand then tugged him into the studio.

Cassie led him over to the painting of Shawn first.

Max was already smiling. "That is wonderful. Shawn looks so strong. Like the perfect Alpha." He lifted a finger before moving it toward the canvas.

"It's still wet," she said, grabbing his hand.

"That's me," Max said. "And Chase and Alex."

"Shawn's inner circle," he told him.

"He's going to love it."

"There's more." She dragged him over to the next easel.

Max gasped.

"The future Alpha," Cassie said. "And his inner circle."

"Alex, Chase, and you." Max took a few steps closer. "Who are the other ones?"

"I don't know," she admitted. "It's just what I saw."

"Thank you." Max turned to her. He pulled Cassie to his chest. "I was having such a hard time seeing myself as the Alpha, as the leader."

"I see it," she whispered. "In my heart, in my head and the inspiration that consumed me. I know you'll do great things."

He brushed his cheek against hers. "I want to do it like you painted. With my inner circle by my side."

Cassie reached up then drew his mouth to hers. "We'll always have your back."

"I love you."

"What?" She jerked back. "Max?"

"Fuck," he muttered. "I didn't mean to blurt it out like that. I was going to take you to dinner then for a ride through the Canyon. I was going to be all romantic and shit."

"I don't care about romance," Cassie told him. "I just want to know you mean it." She gripped the front of his shirt. Cassie shook him. "Tell me that you really mean it."

"Of course I do." He covered her fists with his. "How could I not? You are the most caring, sweet, talented and beautiful person I've ever met."

Cassie sniffed. She would not cry even if Max had just given her everything she'd ever wanted. Love and a future. "You love me."

"I do." Max nodded.

"I love you too," she announced. "More than anything."

"Thank God." Max embraced her before kissing her deeply and thoroughly.

Cassie gave herself over to him. While he carried her toward her the bedroom Max wasn't the future Alpha. He was just the man that she loved. The one that she wanted to spend the rest of her life learning about. The man who was her future.

"I'll protect you," he murmured as he kissed her neck. He laid her down on the mattress before straightening. "I promise to always keep your needs and those of our Pack ahead of my own."

She stared up at him. Cassie wanted to tell him that all the declarations weren't needed. She trusted him.

"I vow to always love you."

Those words were all she needed to hear. "Please." Cassie reached out for him.

Max caught her hand and brought it up to his mouth. "Yes." He winked then covered her body with his.

They'd go to dinner, then take a ride in the canyon. But Cassie was indeed getting her dessert first.

Want to see more from this author?
Here's a taster for you to enjoy!

Bloodlines: Bite
Crissy Smith

Excerpt

Away from the bright lights of the Las Vegas strip, Kieran Smith walked down the dark and litter-ridden street in the roughest part of town. Most tourists didn't see this side of the city but Kieran wasn't like other tourists. He knew he should be in his hotel room steaming in a hot shower or down in the casino spending some of his hard-earned money, but instead he'd strolled for a few hours until he'd found himself far away from the crowds.

Even though the city was well known for sin, there were still different types of vices. The people who had darker and exclusive ones wouldn't be found in the middle of crowds wearing Bermuda shorts with long socks and wielding cameras. No, Kieran had to search out what most people hid from.

He wasn't opposed to sin, necessarily. True he'd spent most of his life protecting those who didn't even know he or his organization existed. But Kieran truly believed that some sins weren't so bad. He strongly believed there were different levels of bad because where was the fun in living if you couldn't enjoy some vices? If he was completely honest with himself, Kieran could admit that he'd left the sanctuary of the safer part of town and was looking for trouble, or more accurately, looking to stop trouble.

He was bored and hadn't seen enough action in the past few weeks. Not since he'd been put on leave along with his partners after an intense case they'd closed with a pack of wolf shifters. Some discreet questioning to the hotel staff where he was staying and Kieran had found where most of the shifters hung around, the ones who caused problems to be more specific. Kieran figured that if any other supernatural types were around, and why wouldn't they be, they'd stay in the same area.

Although he wasn't picky about who or what he captured, his first choice was always shifters. Other than Remy, who'd been one of his work partners for the last several years, Kieran hated all shifters.

If possible, he'd wipe every single one of them off the face of the earth. Unfortunately, as part of the Organization, his job was to protect innocents. It didn't matter if they were human, shifter or like him. Unless they'd committed a crime, they were off limits to him. He really hated that rule.

Kieran had gone through hell when a pack of shifters had captured him after seeing him feed. They'd tortured, experimented on and almost killed him as they'd imprisoned him for over ten years. If it weren't for the Organization getting wind of the lab that had become the only home he could remember, and rescuing him, Kieran knew he wouldn't have made it much longer. Rescue had come but without anywhere to go, he'd been taken in by the people who'd saved him. Although Kieran didn't have the bloodline, like those who were normally chosen to serve as one of the Organization's agents, he'd volunteered to join anyway.

Caspar, the only man who Kieran had trusted for a long time, had put him through training until Kieran had been ready to join the ranks. That was when he'd become partners with Angel, another Day Walker like him, and Remy, the wolf shifter who'd became his best friend. His life had changed due to the Organization, even if everyone other than his boss and two partners thought him crazy. Because of course, he was.

Not only was he a Day Walker that drank blood and fought evil on a daily basis but Kieran was also afraid of the dark, doctors and anything he couldn't control.

All in all, Kieran didn't mind being the psycho of the good guys. He was the monster that parents used in stories to scare their kids into behaving. Only he was very real.

If he hadn't become one of the good guys, there was no telling what he'd have done. So it was a good thing that Caspar had decided he was worth keeping around. Because Kieran would make a really good bad guy, and he knew it.

There were times like tonight when Kieran knew he was standing on the edge between doing the right thing and letting the darkness inside him finally come out. He was barely hanging on to the little sanity he had so he'd gone out hunting for trouble even though he was supposed to be on vacation.

However, after two hours of stalking the streets, Kieran hadn't run into any trouble or even seen another supernatural creature. A few humans were scattered around—most appeared homeless and down on their luck, but there was nothing that required his talents.

Resigned to another night of hanging around the smoky casino floor instead of having any fun, Kieran took the next left at the corner and headed back toward his temporary home. Could a hotel be considered a home? He guessed it didn't really matter. Kieran didn't especially want to be anywhere, so this was as good a place as any. His boss had suggested Las Vegas as one of his vacation spots, thinking that Kieran wouldn't stand out as much here as he normally did. Not that it was Kieran's fault. If they'd wanted him to behave, they shouldn't have sent him on vacation. He didn't care if his partners needed time off. Kieran was lost when he didn't have a purpose.

A scream pierced the quiet night and Kieran froze. He concentrated on the sound to narrow down where it had come from. The empty streets and alleys could cause noise to echo. But Kieran was good at what he did. He took off, using his super-speed to close the distance between him and whoever needed his help. He skidded around an old brick building, which led him into a dark alley. With his excellent night vision, Kieran didn't have any trouble spotting the young couple, a male and female, backed into a wall while three hulking figures closed in on them.

The female screamed again while the attackers laughed at her.

"Hey." Kieran barely raised his voice. If these guys were supernatural, he wouldn't need to. Just as he'd expected, they turned toward him while still keeping their prey in their sights. "Having a party?" Kieran asked with his friendliest tone.

The biggest of the three, an ugly mountain of a man, snarled at him.

Kieran sniffed. It was shifters he'd deal with tonight, oh goody. Kieran could scent the animal part of them clearly. They smelled like wet cat, so feline shifters were on the menu. Depending on what species they were, Kieran could probably figure on a pretty damn good fight. He rubbed his hands together in anticipation.

"Get lost," Mountain Man warned him. He was scenting Kieran and frowning. The shifter wouldn't be able to figure out why Kieran didn't carry any smell except for what he'd picked up from his environment. It was also fun when his opposition had no idea what he was. "Now," the man grumbled.

"I can't do that," Kieran replied with cheer. "I don't think your friends wanted an invite but I do."

"Mind your own business," a second man, small, face like a rat, demanded.

Kieran laughed. "Damn, I don't think I've seen three uglier men in my life. And I've lived a pretty long time." He was giving them hints that he wasn't just another human. With witnesses he couldn't reveal his true nature. His kind wasn't well known and there was a reason for that.

The youngest looking, who had chocolate puppy-dog eyes, was the only one who appeared wary of him. Kieran moved forward slowly the entire time he taunted the shifters, and the youngest was stepping back. Now he was only about six feet away. He glanced over at the couple who were watching him with wide eyes. He waved his hand to them. "Come here," he ordered.

The woman started toward him but the rat man stepped in front of her. "I don't think so. They're ours."

"Not anymore," Kieran said. He leaped up and over the heads of the attackers. He knew he'd taken them by surprise when he was able to shove the rat man forward, sending him flying. Puppy Dog was the first to move but instead of coming at Kieran, he jumped back. Kieran grinned. "I'd get out of here if you don't want to get really hurt," Kieran advised.

Mountain Man growled and lunged at him. Kieran evaded his meaty hand and kicked out, catching his attacker in the knee. The big man went down. That was when the others came at him at the same time. Guess Puppy Dog had grown balls or at least enough to team up with Rat Man. Kieran's training took over. He yelled for the couple to run while he blocked, punched and fought until he was the only one standing. Breathing heavily, he rested his hands on his knees as he stood over his three fallen foes.

That had been fun. He pulled out his phone and hit the pre-dialed number for dispatch. "Clean up on aisle two," he said when the call connected.

"Damn it, Kieran," Lettie Sanchez muttered in his ear. "You're supposed to be on vacation."

"I am on vacation," he argued. "It's not my fault this time."

Lettie snorted. "Trouble just finds you? More like you go looking for it."

It was scary how well Lettie and his other friends knew him. He didn't respond since he really couldn't deny her claim without lying, and he always tried to tell the truth no matter what the circumstances were. He had enough negative traits without adding being a liar as well.

"I've traced the GPS on your phone and am calling in the local agents. Are the suspects secured?" Lettie questioned.

Kieran nudged the ribs of Mountain Man with the toe of his black combat book. "I don't think they're going to be a problem."

"They're not dead, are they?"

He chuckled. "No, there's too much paperwork for dead bodies." And wasn't that the truth. He could remember when the Organization hadn't been so picky about how he took care of threats. But now, they'd gone all politically correct and shit. He suspected that the new views had something to do with the fact that the shifters had gone public and now everyone knew about them. That wasn't something that he worried too much about, though. Above his pay grade.

"How many?" Lettie asked.

"Three," he said with some pride. Kieran might be one of the oldest agents, even if he appeared to be in his early thirties, but he still had it. He could still throw down with the best of them.

Lettie sighed heavily. "When is Angel returning from her honeymoon? She's the only one who can deal with your crazy ass."

"Not for another two weeks," Kieran answered. "Guess you're stuck with me until then."

"Where's Remy?" Lettie questioned. "Sometimes he can be a good influence." Which was sort of true. Mostly, though, Kieran ended up getting both him and Remy in trouble.

"We're on vacation," Kieran reminded her. "He's home with his pack. I'm spending all my money at the tables."

"If that was the case, you wouldn't be calling me to clean up another one of your messes," Lettie pointed out.

Kieran strolled away from the men, who were out cold and who would no doubt remain that way until others arrived. He jumped up and landed on the edge of a graffiti-painted concrete wall before he sat to wait. "You could come down and keep me company."

"Oh, what a wonderful offer. Not," Lettie teased. "I haven't done anything to deserve that kind of punishment."

The banter between them was familiar and finished out his night pretty well. Lettie had been around about half the time he had but they'd connected from the start. She loved electronics as much as he did and was always showing him new inventions she'd come up with. Kieran always took them out to the field and tested them for her. All without their boss knowing because he wouldn't be happy.

"I hear a vehicle approaching," he said. "I'll catch you later, babe." He hung up before she could respond but that was usual for him and he secretly thought Lettie enjoyed his antics.

Kieran stayed where he was, high on the fence, hidden in the dark. A black SUV with heavily tinted windows rolled into the alley. With the headlights bright into the small space, the bodies would be easily seen. Both doors opened, the driver male and passenger female exiting.

"Fuck," the man cursed. When he moved away from the open door, he had his weapon drawn. He was staring at the three men laid out.

Kieran had to smile. He'd enjoy fucking with this agent.

The woman was more cautious. She slowly walked to the front of the vehicle but her eyes were darting around the alley. She wasn't looking at the attackers but instead for who had taken them down. He respected that vigilance. It was what he would do.

He silently rose as he watched. They hadn't spotted him yet. The man was human but the woman was a shifter. It was hard not to snarl at her but he managed. Kieran bent his knees before he leaped down. He landed between them with a loud thud. He ducked slightly when both weapons were pointed at his head. He held up his hands. "Don't shoot," he mocked.

"Kieran Smith." The man lowered his weapon. "I've heard about you, been warned really."

Kieran grinned then glanced at the woman since she hadn't lowered her weapon. "Gonna shoot me?"

"I haven't decided, like my partner said, we've heard about you," she said.

He couldn't really argue with her logic. "Just don't aim for my face. It's too pretty to be shot off."

It was slight but he saw her lips twitch in amusement. And what lips they were—full, plump and red. *Shit!* Where had that thought come from? There was no way in hell that he'd ever find a shifter attractive. Even if the shifter in question had a curvy body, long brown hair streaked with red, and gorgeous bright gold eyes. He'd never seen that color before, but no matter what, Kieran would not think she was hot. No, no way would he ever find a shifter sexy.

"So what happened here?" the male agent asked.

"These three assholes had a couple up against the wall." He waved his hand back as he spoke. "I came along and showed them the error of their ways."

"You took on three shifters all by yourself?" she questioned in disbelief as she strolled closer to the men on the floor. She bent and sniffed.

Kieran grinned. "I thought you'd heard of me?" Lettie had either warned the two agents about him or his reputation was growing. Kieran wasn't sure which he preferred.

"Okay, on that note, I'm Dean Westbridge and this is my partner, Dakota Reese, and we'll be taking over here."

"Dean and Dakota, that's so cute!" Kieran couldn't help but say. Did the Organization chapter here put agents together alphabetically?

Dean snorted. "You really are an asshole."

"Well, Dean Westbridge…" Kieran stopped. *Westbridge?* "Ah fuck!"

"Maybe you're not as slow as you seem," Dakota commented as she rolled the Mountain Man over and secured his hands behind his back with plastic cuffs.

Kieran peered back at Dean, unsure of his next action. *Things just got real interesting.*

The Organization ran off bloodlines. That was how agents were chosen and why they were able to remain secret. The first born, male or female, were sent into service, and very rarely was anyone else ever allowed to even know about their existence. The Westbridges were one of the original families who had formed the Organization. It was also the bloodline that Caspar had been born into. Part of an agreement the founders had made centuries ago. So Dean was related to Kieran's boss — the man he loved like a father. This wasn't good. He'd been hoping to avoid being on Caspar's radar while he was supposed to be taking time off.

"By the look on your face, I'm guessing you've figured out who my uncle is," Dean said. "And if I'm remembering the last conversation I had with him, Caspar told me that you would be in town and to keep an eye on you."

Like he needed a fucking babysitter? Kieran scowled. "Then you haven't been doing a very good job," he taunted. "I've been in town for several days and haven't seen you until tonight."

"But that doesn't mean I haven't seen you. Or how you drink way too much at the hotel bar before dropping several hundred dollars at blackjack?"

"I'm a gambler at heart," he quipped. How hadn't he seen this man watching him? Well actually, Kieran knew. He didn't give humans a second look. They were no threat to him. Kieran was untouchable. Or at least he'd always believed he was. This human male might be a challenge. Kieran turned his back to Dean, showing him that he didn't find him any danger. Dakota had bound the mountain man, the rat guy, and was now bending over the young puppy-dog-eyed kid.

Kieran strolled over to her with his hands in the pockets of his dark jeans. "That one's not much more than a kid. He couldn't fight off a tick. Do shifters get fleas and ticks?" he baited her.

Dakota glanced up at him. "Could you be any more obvious?" she asked.

He lifted an eyebrow.

"Fine." She finished securing the attacker then stood. "You can continue to play your games and push away everyone you meet. If that's the way you want to play it, we can't stop you. But maybe you should ask yourself why Caspar suggested you take the rest of your vacation here?"

"He likes to screw with my head," he replied with a shrug.

"Sure." She patted his chest before resting her palm over his heart.

The heat from her hand seeped through his cotton T-shirt and he froze. For the first time in many years, his instinct was not to rip off the head of the shifter who touched him. Instead he ached to pull her close. He shook his head to gather control of himself.

"I can see you've got this under control," he murmured. Then he sped off. Kieran put every ounce of his energy in getting away from Dakota.

He had a hotel to check out of and another lodging to find. Dean might have been given the task of watching out for him but Kieran wouldn't make it easy for him.

So let the games begin.

Dakota grinned as Kieran disappeared almost right before her eyes. "Damn, he's fast."

"And you need to be careful. Caspar specifically told us that Kieran hates shifters and that he'd like nothing more than to kill you," Dean told her. "You shouldn't have touched him."

Probably, but she hadn't been able to help herself. It was so obvious that Kieran used his sharp tongue to push others away. He didn't want people close to him but there was also a longing for connection deep inside him that she could sense. It was her job to read people—what she'd specialized in during training. Kieran Smith was so much more than what he appeared.

"Maybe you should stay away from him. I can have Gabe help me follow him," Dean said.

"No." While Kieran might have issues, it hadn't been hate that she'd seen in his eyes. The spark of attraction had been unmistakable. He wasn't exactly what she'd been expecting either so she'd paid attention to every detail. "I'm not backing off."

When she'd touched him, he'd been shocked. Kieran's body had been hard and cool but his eyes had been full of heat.

"Shit," Dean muttered. "You have that look on your face."

"What look?" she asked with fake innocence.

"The one that says you've found a lost puppy to bring home," he said.

She'd laugh, but he wasn't too far off. Kieran needed to know that someone cared for him. He was lost in his own world and very alone. It wasn't in Dakota to leave someone to flounder about. The fact that she was attracted to him just added to her need to care for him. Whether he liked it or not.

A groan sounded from behind as she whirled around. The biggest of the shifters was waking up. "Let's get these guys processed so we can get back to your secret mission," she said.

"I can't believe I let Caspar talk me into watching him," Dean bitched.

"Like you'd ever say no to Caspar," she said. Caspar was better to Dean than Dean's own father. Because of the respect Dean had for his uncle, there was no doubt that he'd do anything Caspar asked. "You know he'll be gone by the time we get done here and back to his hotel."

"Yeah," Dean agreed. "Let's get these three loaded and I'll call Gabe to stake him out. He won't leave town so we'll find him."

"Maybe," Dakota said, not really agreeing. Now that Kieran knew they were watching him, there was no telling what he would do. She didn't think he'd just disappear, though. His personality made her think he'd try to make it really hard to keep their promise to watch him. Kieran would probably do his best to show them up.

"I'll get the little guy," Dean said as he walked to the youngest of their prisoners.

"Thanks," she grumbled as she strode to the largest man, and the only one who was awake. "Hey." She lightly kicked his side. "Get up."

The man scowled at her. "Who the fuck are you?"

Dakota dropped to her knees in front of him. She let her jaguar come close to the surface. She had a powerful animal inside her, and the way the guy's eyes widened, she knew he hadn't been prepared for the wave of dominance that she released. "Any more questions?" she growled.

He shook his head.

As she climbed to her feet, she grabbed his arm and hauled him up. Dean had already carried the smallest to the back of their SUV and was now headed in her direction. She pushed her detainee toward Dean before turning to the last guy. He was scrawny and damn ugly. No wonder he'd turned to a life of crime. Dakota bent to lift him up and threw him over her shoulder.

Dean just shook his head at her. It was an ongoing joke between them that she did most of the heavy lifting and that he was the brains in their partnership. Sure, it had something to do with her shifter strength, but really Dakota enjoyed showing off her muscles and Dean was really smart. They worked well together.

She carried the last suspect to the SUV, then Dean helped her get him inside.

"You drive," Dean said as he circled around the back of the vehicle. "I'll make the phone calls to track down our wayward Walker." It was the first time Dean had brought up what Kieran was.

"Have you ever met a Walker before now?" she asked as she slammed the back door shut. She climbed into the driver's seat and started the SUV.

"No," Dean said as he joined her. "There are just so few of them. My dad, and of course Caspar, talks about some of the older ones but I've never come face to face with anyone like Kieran before."

She hadn't either. "I've read a lot of reports involving Day Walkers," she said. "I wonder how much is true and how much they put into the reports to keep their secrets."

"I would think if the information comes from our files, it would be pretty accurate," Dean told her.

"I don't know," she argued. "Wouldn't it make more sense to only put in the details they don't mind us knowing about?"

"They've been around too long for the Organization not to know almost everything," he told her.

"Okay." She put their SUV into reverse and started to back out of the alley. She still thought her partner was wrong but only time would tell. The more she could watch Kieran, the better idea she would have about how Walkers worked.

Beside her, Dean was speaking to Gabe about arranging a more detailed surveillance on Kieran. Gabe worked on a team with Dare, a bear shifter, and Riley, a fox shifter. Their team backed her and Dean the most. There were currently four squads of agents in the Las Vegas area. Her boss, Marcello Sparro, had concerns about the number of supernaturals who were arriving in town. There was talk about recruiting more agents.

Secretly that was the reason that Kieran had been directed to vacation here. Dakota didn't know why Caspar wouldn't just tell Kieran what was going on. Instead Caspar had told Kieran he needed time off, and told Dean to keep an eye on the Walker. She wondered what else they didn't know.

As she drove south, heading to the Organization headquarters, she kept her eye out for Kieran. There was a good chance that he might follow them. To her knowledge, Kieran didn't know where their office was located, and that information would be beneficial to him to find if he was planning anything against them. It wasn't like he'd be able to type them into a Google search or look for them in the phone book. They didn't exist to the outside world.

While the general public might be aware that shifters existed, they had no clue what still remained in the shadows. Day Walkers were the closest thing to what people would call vampires. Yes, Walkers drank blood, had superior senses and were the scariest in the supernatural world, but they were also the rarest. And all the myths about vampires and how to kill them were pretty much bullshit from what her research had shown. Crosses, garlic and wooden stakes had no more control over them than they would on a human or shifter.

It was interesting the way humans had accepted shifters easily enough and yet had never thought to ask what else was out there.

Dakota made a left on Falcon Ave, which would lead her right into the underground parking garage of the Murphy Institute — the cover corporation for the Las Vegas Organization's units.

The Murphy Institute took half a block and rose three stories high. The dark brick hid one of the most advanced businesses in the country. Everything inside, from the labs, temporary housing and lock-up to the sleek offices were all state of the art. It could be a little intimidating the first time someone walked through the doors but Dakota loved it there. It sure as hell beat her training days of camping out for months at a time, constant cold and wetness, and the dorms she'd grown up living in.

Unlike most of her coworkers, Dakota lived on site. She didn't see the point of getting her own place, since at any time she could be sent away for a temporary assignment or for a permanent relocation. Why get comfortable when in a second she could be gone? Her partner was the total opposite but he had more contact with his family than most agents.

Dakota hadn't spoken to her parents or siblings since she was a teenager. It was just too hard to hear about how well her family was doing when she'd never be allowed to join them. She had five siblings, two of whom she'd never even met. Not that she didn't keep an eye on them, but she kept it strictly to her files and under surveillance. She made no effort to contact them and they didn't even seem to think about her, ever.

She shook her depressing thoughts away. This was her life, and for the most part, she enjoyed what she did. As the eldest child, it was her duty to follow the agreement that her ancestors had made. She was a third-generation agent and her family depended on her to watch out for the innocent.

"We're here," she told Dean as she slowed to a stop at the guard gate leading into the underground parking. Her vehicle was equipped with a tracking device and a bar scan on the window so the sensors could pick her up, but she still had to show her ID to get inside.

She rolled down her window before she flipped open her identification. "Hey, Margie," she greeted the guard on duty.

"Hi, Dakota, Dean." Margie walked up to the driver side. She peered in the back. "Three?" she asked.

"Yes," Dakota confirmed. "We'll take them directly to the third-floor lock-up."

Since the shifter suspects had targeted humans, her and Dean's job was to get them processed so the law-enforcement agents could be informed. They'd call in either the local police or use the newly formed Shifter Coalition, depending on how severe the crime was.

With these three jokers, Dakota guessed it would be the locals who would have to come pick them up.

The Shifter Coalition worked more like the FBI or Homeland Security but was run entirely by shifters. Their presence was common knowledge as shifters had publically started the agency so that humans knew nonhumans were being policed as well. Dakota had only met a couple of Coalition agents since they'd opened an office close by but those she'd met seemed to be good people. It didn't bother her that they were in her town. It actually helped. While the Coalition took the more public cases and had to work within human laws, Dakota and the Organization could continue to slink around in the shadows.

"This is it," she said to her passengers.

"Where are we and what in the hell was that man earlier? He wasn't a shifter and he sure wasn't human," the big guy asked.

Dakota glanced up into the rear-view mirror so she could see his eyes. "This is the final stop of our tour. You'll be passed off to the cops from here."

"Cops!" he shouted. "I should be the one pressing charges. That man was a lunatic."

"That man could have killed you and no one would have ever known," Dakota said honestly. "Instead he called for us to pick you up. You should count yourself lucky."

The prisoner snorted. "Yeah right."

"And if you know what's good for you," Dean added, looking over into the back seat, "you'll make sure your paths never cross again."

Dakota pressed her lips tight to hide her smile. The way all three prisoners paled spoke volumes.

"What was he?" the youngest looking asked in a whisper.

"You best pray you never find out," she warned.

He nodded frantically.

About the Author

Crissy Smith lives in Texas with her husband, daughter, and three Labrador retrievers. The three dogs love to curl up under her computer desk and nap while she writes. It doesn't leave a lot of room for her but what's a woman to do?

When not writing or reading, she enjoys hunting, camping and shooting. But she has a girly side too and is addicted to pedicures and coffee.

She has been writing since she was a teenager and still loves everything to do with the paranormal. Her stories and characters all have a place in her heart. She loves the Alpha male, the dominant werewolf, and the Master vampire, which find their way in most of her books.

Learn more about the characters she has created at her website where they have their very own page. It will be updated from time to time to let you know what's going on with them. Also you can find out who will be in the next book.

Crissy loves to hear from readers. You can find her contact information, website details and author profile page at http://www.totallybound.com.